AVENGER

The Bugging Out Series: Book Six

NOAH MANN

ISBN-10: 1539795780
ISBN-13: 978-1539795780

Before you embark
on a journey of revenge,
dig two graves.

Confucius

Part One

Discontent

One

The body washed ashore sometime in the night as snow blew in from an arctic front battering the coast. While a detail was dragging it up from the surf line they spotted another. Then another. And another.

"Forty," Sergeant Lorenzen reported just after dawn broke.

Standing next to me on the beach road, Captain Angela Schiavo nodded at the grim statistic and watched her second in command hustle back down toward the churning water where a dozen residents of Bandon were dragging and stacking the corpses like wood for the winter.

Death had come to our town again.

"The storm got them," I said, looking through the swirling blizzard to the contradiction before us—the violent Pacific. "Out there."

"Who are they?" Schiavo wondered, the rhetorical musing spoken without expectation of any accurate answer.

"If we've pulled forty from the water, there's at least double that we'll never find."

Schiavo didn't doubt my estimation. The churning sea had already swallowed those who hadn't remained afloat long enough to be swept ashore.

"They had a boat," Schiavo said. "A big one."

A hundred or more passengers. Plus supplies. How large the craft needed to be depended much on how far the unlucky souls had traveled, or planned to travel. The unlikely storm, hammering our town for three days now, had dumped six inches of snow, an uncommon occurrence for the coast this far south. The winds, at times, had reached gale force, heaving huge waves that fought the outflowing current of the Coquille River, threatening to undo the repairs only recently completed to the town's harbor. Boats that had been refloated and salvaged were thrown against their moorings. It wasn't the first bout of fierce weather we'd been faced with, but we had, so far, come through it relatively unscathed.

Relatively...

Storms weren't the only events we'd weathered. Difficulties, both large and small, had tested us. Struggles. Sickness. Loss.

I let my gaze settle on Schiavo. On her profile. She stared out at the raging ocean, the icy blow chapping her cheeks. It seemed to me, though, that she was looking beyond the physical world. Beyond the cold, soaking death washing up on our beach. Thinking not of those who'd left this life out there, but of one who had never arrived.

Six months it had been since the miscarriage. Since she had lost the baby she and Martin had, unexpectedly, planned to welcome into the world. Hardly two months after we'd driven off the Unified Government forces laying siege to our town, Schiavo had fallen ill. At first there was some fear that the virus released by our enemy had returned. Soon, though, what had truly occurred became apparent.

She'd never expected to be expecting, I recalled her telling me, standing on this very beach, when Bandon was surrounded. But the sudden loss of her child, of their child, had, nonetheless, stolen something from her. From them. A chance at something new. Something good. Possibly the best thing—new, innocent life.

"If these people made it, then others did," Schiavo observed.

Old life. Survivors of the blight. That was what she was referring to. Others had persevered. Struggled. Lived. Maybe even thrived. In death, be it singular or en masse, one could deduce that there was still life to behold. Still hope.

Hope...

"But where the hell did they come from?"

Her question was obvious. But I wondered if it even mattered.

"Why would they be out there?" Schiavo wondered, looking to me now. "I mean right out there. There's no decomposition. They had to drown near here. Near us."

I knew what she was suggesting with her question—that the victims of the storm being dragged from the water had intended to travel here.

"We were their destination," I said.

Schiavo nodded.

"Who knows we're here, Fletch?"

Before I had a chance to reply, Sergeant Lorenzen approached, something in hand. More than one something. Wallets. In those, our unspoken suspicions were confirmed.

"These were on three of the male victims," he said.

He held them out. Schiavo and I each took one, unfolding the soaked vestiges of the world long gone. Identification and money, both plastic and paper, had once filled the leather and fabric slots within. And, oddly, some still held onto those reminders of their past lives, just as my Elaine still had her FBI credentials.

And as Neil, my friend, had retained his passport. A memento of his travels. Of the false life he'd led.

I forced those thoughts down. In the month after his death, his murder, I'd dwelt on all things related to his life, and to mine, where the two intersected. Every inconsistency vexed me. Every half-truth that I berated myself for not recognizing.

Then, with help, I stopped. I let go.

'You kill him again and again every moment you obsess over what you didn't know.'

That was what Elaine had said to me.

'Remember the life he shared with you, not the one he hid.'

Her words were wise, and following their directive was not easy, but follow them I did. Despite momentary diversions into wonder about this aspect, or that facet, of the unknown world my friend had inhabited as an intelligence operative, the vast majority of my memories of Neil Moore lived on as snippets of our happy times together. High school. Hunting. Fishing. Friendship.

"San Diego," Schiavo said. "Arthur Horton."

I had the wallet I'd picked open before me, and was seeing what the captain was.

"David Juarez," I read. "San Diego address."

"This one has a Utah address," Lorenzen said, showing the wallet he'd retained. "But I remember this name—Luther Lukins."

I recalled it, too. It was unique enough, in a lyrically spoken sort of way, that it was imprinted in my memory the first time I'd heard it. In Skagway.

"They're from San Diego," I said.

The San Diego survivor colony. I couldn't recall how many had been rescued in Skagway along with those from Edmonton and Yuma, in addition to our own friends and loved ones from Bandon. The number was in the hundreds. And now, as it appeared, they were gone. Wiped out while seeking safety. While seeking freedom.

Schiavo looked out into the storm again, as did Lorenzen and I.

"I imagine we know where the Unified Government forces redeployed after they left us," she said.

"They were running," Lorenzen said.

"If they were surrounded like we were, the ocean was their only avenue of retreat," Schiavo agreed.

"They have Yuma," I said, recalling our brief contact via radio with that survivor colony that confirmed a takeover by the Unified Government. "If San Diego is gone, that leaves Edmonton."

"We've had no contact with them," Lorenzen said. "Mo and Krista have been trying daily."

Private 'Mo not Morris' Westin, the garrison's communications specialist, had recently begun receiving relief in those duties from a likely, and unlikely, source. The time Krista had spent with Micah before the boy's passing, as well as her use of Del's radio at my Montana refuge, had afforded her an accelerated lesson in the use of the boy's communication tools, and the computers used to monitor and control them. In the wake of Neil's death, and her mother's quiet, stoic grieving for him, the girl had shifted her focus from artistic endeavors to more technical activities to occupy herself. At twelve years old she'd taken on a role, voluntarily, that those twice her age would struggle with.

"It could just be distance," I said. "The radio signal, mountains. A lot could go wrong before they ever hear us."

With the Ranger Signal long gone, as were its predecessors which had choked the airwaves, communication by radio was possible again. Short range units had been functioning in our town for months. As for what was working elsewhere...

"No one's hearing us," Schiavo said.

I knew who she meant. Washington. Or Hawaii. The two places she knew that our government, the rightful government, had been functioning in some capacity. Whether that still held true was beyond our ability to know at the moment.

"Or they're just not there to respond," Lorenzen suggested.

Whatever the reason, we were, as far as any of us could deduce, on our own.

The radio on Schiavo's hip beeped, an alert tone indicating that a communication was waiting. She took it in hand and held it close to her face to shield it from the gusting flurries.

"This is the captain."

"Ma'am, is Fletch with you?"

It was Westin. A usually calm voice when communicating, his tone on the radio now hinted at some urgency, and that made me turn toward the captain and step close, wanting, needing to hear what was being said.

"He's right here," Schiavo reported.

"Get him to the hospital," Westin said. "Fast."

My heart sank. The sudden fear that I felt was not a solitary experience. Both Schiavo and Lorenzen eyed me with instant worry.

"What is it?" Schiavo asked.

"Neighbors just brought Elaine in," Westin reported. "Her water broke."

Two

"God, no, it hurts!"

I held Elaine's hand and let her bear down upon it as another wave of pain, of agony, washed over her.

"You're doing fine," I told her. "You're doing so great."

Just to my left, Commander Clay Genesee sat on a stool between my wife's splayed legs, stirrups holding them apart. Across from me, her attention shifting between a trio of monitors registering various vital signs, Grace held Elaine's other hand. I kept looking to her, to my friend's widow, soaking in her strength and searching for clues as to just how much danger my wife was in.

The baby wasn't due for another three weeks. We'd expected that we would have that time to complete preparations for the child whose conception was a surprise, but not a shock. Having a child, starting a family, was a desire we'd talked about, thought on, but never acted on affirmatively. But, like Martin and Angela's pregnancy, this reality had come in its own time.

I only hoped that we would not face the heartbreak which they had.

"I need you to breathe, Elaine," Genesee said. "Breathe and don't push."

"Ahhhhhhhhhhhh!"

The cry she let out was a mix of pain and compliance as she resisted the overpowering urge to bear down. To get the child out of her. To end the agony.

"Grace," Elaine said, looking up to our friend after a deep breath. "Is the baby all right?"

The baby...

In the old world we might have known all there was to know about the child we were about to have. Its gender, genetic abnormalities, anticipated weight. On the *Rushmore's* first visit to Bandon, the Navy ship had offloaded a collection of medical supplies to accompany Commander Genesee, including medicines and equipment necessary to handle the expected arrivals of new life. We'd had an ultrasound, several, in fact, but the uncooperative child my wife carried had never allowed a proper vantage to determine its sex. So it was just *'the baby'*. Not *'him'*, or *'her'*.

"The baby is doing fine," Grace said, looking away from the monitors and focusing on Elaine. "And you're doing amazing."

It might have been the reassurance, or the bolstering compliment, but at that instant Elaine burst into tears. A brief sobbing, both appreciative and fearful.

"But it's early..."

Grace leaned close, still holding my wife's hand, and fixed a forceful, certain gaze on her.

"Your baby is a trooper," Grace assured her. "Remember the ultrasounds?"

Elaine nodded, the tears stopped now, just remnants on her cheeks.

"Doctor Genesee said your little one was a bruiser at thirty-two weeks," Grace reminded her. "Your due date could be a tad off."

Again, Elaine nodded, the words calming her, as did the obvious truth they told. We could have gotten pregnant earlier, throwing off the estimate. And the last ultrasound did show a well-developed child, and a sizeable one at that. Her worry, our worry, could be simply unfounded.

But she could not relax, nor could I, until we both saw our child, and heard it, and held it, and knew that we'd brought a healthy baby into the world. Into this world that needed it so much.

"Ahhhhhhhh!"

A sudden wave of pain ended the calming exchange, Elaine squeezing my hand, and Grace's, with almost painful force.

"Okay, Elaine," Genesee said past the half sheet draped over her knees. "One big push when I tell you, okay?"

"Okay, okay, okay."

My wife breathed, fast and focused, wanting to push, fighting the pain, holding back the irresistible urge until the word was given.

"Now, Elaine," Genesee said. "A big push. A big one."

Elaine curled forward, her face twisted, Grace and I supporting her as she bore down, muscles contracting, an almost pitiful, exhausted cry slipping past her lips. It was the only sound in the room for a moment until we heard another cry. A tiny, strong, wonderful cry.

"Ahhhhhh," Elaine half sighed, half screamed, collapsing back against the raised head of the bed. Grace pulled her hand free of Elaine's grip and stepped close to Genesee, taking a sterile scissors from a tray of waiting instruments.

"You did it," I said, leaning close and planting a kiss on Elaine's glistening forehead. "You're amazing."

She smiled through tears of exhausted joy, then tried to lift herself to see down between her splayed legs. Something small there was wailing. Our child. Announcing its presence. Out of view.

"Is everything okay?" Elaine asked, eager but not worried. "Is he...she...okay?"

There was a metallic snip out of view, the newborn wailing before, during, and after the cutting of its umbilical cord. Its last hard connection to the wonderful mother who had carried it had been severed.

It...

I couldn't continue thinking of our child in that generic way.

"Clay, what is it?"

He heard my question, but did not immediately answer. His hands worked, in concert with Grace's, manipulating, tying, suctioning, cleaning, injecting, and finally wrapping our child out of view. Then, he rose slowly from the stool on which he'd sat, a white bundle in hand. He passed it to Grace, and she came up the side of the birthing bed, placing the tiny new life upon Elaine's chest.

"Say hello to your daughter," Genesee said, allowing a thin but very true smile.

"Daughter..."

The word came out mostly as breath, but not because of any surprise, or disappointment. It was simply that we now had more than a 'child'. We had a daughter. A little girl.

"Hey, sweetie," Elaine said, bringing her close to her face and planting a soft kiss on our girl's forehead.

I did the same, my cheeks pressed to my wife's.

"A little girl," Elaine said, angling her head to look at me. "A girl."

"That's what all the parts tell me," Genesee said.

I looked up to the doctor. To the man who'd come to Bandon not wanting to be in Bandon. A man whose tenure had alternated between contentious and resigned. He'd been aloof. He'd been suspect.

But he'd slowly become one of us. Within, he longed for the old world. I knew this, though he never talked of the time before the blight tore civilization asunder and defiled the life he'd known. Not when probed directly, nor through innocent conversation. Others, too, had held close what they'd been through. What they lost. People I'd come to know, and to respect. Burke Stovich was one. And I was beginning to suspect that, whether he could imagine it or not, Commander Clay Genesee was another.

"We'll get you into a room in a few minutes," Genesee said, glancing to Grace.

"It's already set up," she told him.

Genesee gave a small nod, that smile still showing, and left the treatment room which had been turned into a labor and delivery suite.

"I'm so happy for you both," Grace said.

Elaine eased one hand from our daughter and reached toward Grace. She leaned down and hugged us both, holding tight, the embrace lingering. There was happiness in the exchange. And sadness. She knew, as did I, that another should be there with us. Sharing this moment. Basking in the joy.

"Neil would be so, so giddy about this," Grace said as she straightened again, just a thin sheen of tears glistening over her eyes. "He would."

"I know," I said.

He was gone. My friend. Murdered in cold blood by a man who had once been a friend and colleague to him. Killed after a selfless act which had saved our town. Our home.

And our lives.

There was still much to be angry about, and in moments when I let the animus rise I could still see the face of Tyler Olin. The face of the man who'd taken my friend from me, taken a husband from Grace, and a father from Brandon and Krista. It was a face I both never wanted to see again, and one I wished was just outside the hospital, within reach, so I could bring vengeance upon the man who'd hurt so many and wronged an entire town.

This, though, was not the moment to entertain such thoughts. This was a moment where new life had presented itself. A good moment. Perfection in the form of a child.

"I'll give you all a while to catch your breaths, then we'll move you," Grace said, then she stepped past the delivery table and into the hallway, closing the door and leaving us alone.

Us...

We were not just a couple anymore. We were more.

We were a family.

It was more than cliché to think what I was, but it was also true. And appropriate. Because for the moment, despite anything that existed beyond the hospital's walls, all was right with the world.

Three

One of the first things I said to Elaine when we were alone with our daughter in a regular room was laughably obvious.

"She's so little."

"Babies are."

"But..."

I didn't know how to express myself yet. Not about this. Not about her.

"I never thought I'd be a father," I said, leaning close to my wife as she cradled our child. "I never thought I'd be married."

Elaine's gaze shifted to me and smiled.

"You never thought the world would end, either."

I allowed a slight chuckle at the observation, incorrect as it was. The world hadn't ended. It had come close. *We* had come close to losing it all. But we'd fought back, in more ways that I could have imagined. Humankind had persevered, even when faced with those who'd lost their humanity.

"Okay," Elaine said, prelude in her tone. "Decision time. She needs a name."

I nodded at the tiny wonder who was our daughter. For whatever reason we hadn't discussed any possible names to choose from. Part of it might have been fear of not having that chance. Fear of something going wrong before our child made its way into this world, screaming and oblivious to what we all faced. That fear had been realized early on for Martin and Angela. Their heartbreak was real, and, almost certainly, it was permanent. Even if they decided to try and conceive again, both Doc Allen and Commander Genesee told them that their chances were slim of successfully carrying a child to term.

But two other women had given birth since the Unified Government forces were driven off. And now there was a third. There was, as my friend had always said, hope.

And in that instant, with that snippet of a warm recollection, I knew.

"Hope," I said.

Elaine looked to me, puzzled at first, wondering why I would bring Neil's mantra into this moment of decision. Then, without me needing to say another word, she smiled, realizing that the single word I'd spoken was the decision.

"Hope," she said, looking down to our swaddled daughter and planting a soft kiss on her wrinkled pink forehead. "What else could it be?"

It wasn't a question she posed. It was a statement of certainty.

"Hope Fletcher," I said.

She was perfect. It was a belief all parents held when gazing upon their newborn child. But here, I knew, she actually was. And the world needed her. It needed more like her. Perfect, unsullied keepers of the flame.

We'd brought green back to the earth turned grey. And now we were bringing life back, little by little. We were warriors and pioneers. Trailblazers. Dreamers.

"Do you—"

The sudden jolt cut off my question. It shook the building, not with any devastating force, but with enough punch to remind us that, even if the surface of the planet had been devastated by man's biological trickery, Mother Nature still ran the show.

"Earthquake," Elaine said, clutching our daughter just that much tighter. "Another one."

Oregon was earthquake country, sitting close to the Pacific ring of fire, a geologic hotbed of colliding tectonic plates out in the ocean to the west. If one forgot that factoid, just walking through town and seeing the fading Tsunami Evacuation Route signs was reminder enough that an upheaval of the ocean floor off shore could send a wall of water racing toward the town.

And, in the past two months, the frequency of tremblors had increased, something those longtime residents of the seaside town said was worrisome, but not any certain harbinger of a major event. My old life in Montana had exposed me to only the most minor of earthquakes, though catastrophic ones had struck that region in the past. Here, though, the earth's violent tendencies were worth taking note of—and being prepared for.

The door opened quickly, though not urgently, Grace stepping in.

"You both all right?"

Elaine smiled and nodded.

"All three of us," she said.

Grace smiled, too, mindful of her innocent mistake.

"That didn't feel *too* big," Grace commented.

There was no functioning Richter scale in town to provide us with an accurate measure of the shakers we'd experienced. Those who'd been through many in the past had said the larger quakes felt somewhere in the low 4 range, with most of less intensity than that.

"Already enough excitement for today," I said.

"Hope's first earthquake," Elaine said.

Still standing near the door, Grace's smile softened, to something more sweet than bitter.

"Hope," she said.

"I don't think there's a better name," Elaine told her. "Not after everything."

Grace didn't say anything for a moment. But it was plain from the pure emotion in her eyes that she could not agree more.

"I guess we should fill out some paperwork on her," Grace said.

Paperwork...

Yes, we were edging back toward some semblance of civilization, with forms and procedures to properly record the arrival of new children. Doing so had been Mayor Allen's idea, though I'd wondered if his suggestion of our adoption of birth certificates was just the machinations of a man, an old man, reaching back for some bit of the past. Particularly with the passing of his wife after the Unified Government's use of its virus to weaken the town. There hadn't been many deaths, but, sadly, Carol Allen had been one.

"Hope," Grace said again. "I'll get the birth certificate and let Commander Genesee know he's got something to sign."

With that she left us. In her absence, as we waited for an official record of her birth to be made, Elaine and I simply looked at our girl. At our Hope. We said nothing. Just stared. Stared at the most wonderful thing either of us had ever seen.

Four

I drove through the storm to gather those things my wife would need for a few days in the hospital.

We'd planned to have her 'go bag' ready the following week, which, we'd believed, was plenty of time. We, and those with medical expertise, had been wrong.

Or, I had to allow, our daughter had just been anxious to make her entrance.

Now, though, as Elaine lay in a hospital bed with Hope in a basinet no more than twelve inches away, I made my way through the swirling snow. At times the rare blizzard spat waves of icy flakes across the road, a horizontal whiteout washing away the roadway and houses to either side as I turned onto our street. The Humvee's headlights reflected off the wall of white, blinding me as I crept the vehicle forward. I killed the lights as I neared our house and eased to the curb.

Wind nearly ripped the door from my hands as I stepped from the vehicle. I leaned my body against it to get it shut, pulling the hood of my parka up, as much to mask the sound of the wailing gusts as to keep me warm. The fury of the historic storm pounded on me as I half stumbled around the front of the Humvee and up the walkway to the porch of our house.

At the bottom step I moved no further, one foot planted on the wooden tread, my gaze peering past the edges of the cinched hood to the window to the left of the front door. I'd seen something there. The silhouette of something.

Of someone.

Instinctively I raised the side of my parka and slipped the Springfield from its holster, keeping the safety on. For the moment. There'd been a number of petty thefts in town over the past month and a half, which some had attributed to bored teenagers seeking thrills in a world where once ubiquitous activities had been erased with most of the technological infrastructure. There were computers, but no vast network which allowed continuous and instant communication with peers, be they fifty feet or ten thousand miles away. Every band they'd followed religiously was gone. Movies no longer showed weekly at the theater in North Bend, twenty miles up the coast, a facility which still stood, but had long ago been looted and vandalized, our scouting missions had confirmed.

I, though, wasn't convinced that simple mischief was behind the minor burglaries. What had been taken didn't seem to fit the act of misguided youth. Essentials were missing. Staples scrounged from our continuous scouting missions, mostly to the south along the coast and inland to the east. Toothpaste, sewing kits, kitchen knives, and the odd can of food were what turned up gone. None of it, not a single item, had been recovered in town, even after Schiavo had Martin interview suspects and perform searches authorized by the Defense Council.

My own suspicion was that someone in town, not a teenager, was gathering the supplies. Stockpiling. Maybe in preparation for another assault like the one we'd been subjected to at the hands of the Unified Government.

As it turned out, I was as wrong as everyone else.

I backed away from the front steps and slipped down the side of the house, carefully high-stepping through low drifts of snow that had piled against the siding nearly halfway up to the windows. In less than half a minute I was near the back door, close enough to see that one small pane in its glass inlay had been broken out. Just a quick reach through would allow any intruder to twist the lock and open the door.

My thumb moved slightly and slid the safety down on my Springfield, making it ready for immediate use, my hold on it already depressing the integral grip safety. I crouched slightly and climbed the back steps, the storm masking any sound my weight might make on the aging treads and risers. I hoped. There could be someone waiting just inside the door, already knowing of my presence and approach. For all I knew a lookout had spotted me as I drove up.

None of those possibilities, though, negated the reality that I had to confront what faced me. There was no 911 to call anymore. At least not yet. There had been some discussion by the Defense Council, spurred by citizen suggestions, to look at forming a police force. Something that would separate the act of enforcing laws from the military component charged with protecting the town from outside threats. It was not a bad goal to work toward, but we were not there yet. Which meant every individual was, in many ways, the only first responder available to maintain law. And order.

With my free hand I gripped the doorknob. Once I turned it and pushed the door open, there would be no doubt of my presence to any inside. The raging wind's roar would signal clearly that the entrance had been breached. I would be committing myself to dealing with whoever, and whatever, was inside.

There was no final, calming breath before I decided. I simply acted, pushing the door inward and stepping through, leaving it open, tendrils of the storm slapping it again and again against the counter inside. To the left was a closet, and past that an opening to the hall and the bedrooms beyond. To my right was the main space of the kitchen, and another pathway to the hall, this one passing through our small dining room. Choosing which way to move took me just a second, and I turned left, exiting the kitchen after just a few steps.

The hallway was empty. Even in the dark of the house I could see that. Enough ambient light was bleeding in through the front windows, as well as those in the bedrooms, to reveal a bare corridor. My next consideration was to decide on an exploration of the bedrooms versus heading straight for the front of the house.

The sound from my left made that choice for me.

Our bedroom...

Not the nursery, which we'd completed painting and furnishing just a few days earlier, but from the room in which Elaine and I slept. There was nothing of value in there. No food, no weapons, the former kept exclusively in the kitchen, and the latter, except for the sidearm I carried, locked in the closet near the front door. From my position I would have seen that space opened in the front room, but it was not.

Click...

That sound now focused my full attention toward our bedroom door. It could have been many things, but what concerned me was its similarity to the sound of a weapon's safety being moved, from safe to fire I had to assume.

Then, I heard something else. Something which should not have surprised me, but which did. A voice. Hushed. Whispering very deliberately.

A woman's voice.

There was just enough timbre audible that I could make such an assumption. Still, if I was correct, who was she whispering to? Another intruder? Herself?

The latter possibility was not as farfetched as it seemed. On treks both to and from Bandon I had crossed paths with survivors whose mental faculties had been more than degraded. After landing our aircraft on the road while seeking out Eagle One, Neil, Grace, Krista, and I had come across a woman who'd cut her own eyelids off. While seeking the source of salvation in Cheyenne, Elaine, Neil, and I witnessed a man in a business suit walking calmly down the road, dead cellphone to his ear. Even in Bandon there were two residents whose peculiar ways sometimes resulted in solitary conversations with themselves.

Both of those locals, though, were men.

I might be facing more than one intruder. That likelihood slowed my advance as I weighed the best course of action. There was retreat, backing carefully out and summoning help, though by the time assistance arrived the house would likely be empty again, those who'd broken in gone into the storm. I didn't want that to happen. I had to know, we had to know, if there were others out there, near our borders, who were raiding our homes and our fields.

The decision I made leaned mostly toward the latter need.

"You're not getting out," I said, holding position, my weapon pointed at the floor near the door to our bedroom. "Walk out of the bedroom with your hands visible."

I silently reprimanded myself for not automatically deploying the small flashlight I carried. A simple tap on its switch as the intruder exited the bedroom would have illuminated the scene properly. But as it was, the small device rested at the bottom of my left front pocket. Reaching for it would have been a simple exercise, but in no way did I want to take the support hand off my weapon. The ambient light would simply have to do.

As it turned out, that was the mistake which turned what should have been a position of advantage to one which could have cost me my life.

I'd expected one of two things to happen—the intruder to emerge with their hands empty and up, as I'd instructed, or total noncompliance in the form of silence, which would have forced me to enter the room to force the issue. The person who'd broken into my house made their own choice.

In a flash of shadows the intruder was through the bedroom door and charging at me in the narrow, darkened hallway. My mind made several quick assumptions based upon the sudden flow of visual data. What appeared to be hands were empty, and the stature of the figure charging me seemed small, or smaller than me. When that appraisal was combined with the voice I'd heard, I was more convinced than ever that the person barreling at me was female.

All of these things kept me from bringing my weapon up and firing. I'd held it low on the off chance that the belief about local teens turned out to be true. There was no way I was going to put a bullet into a kid unless I was forced to. The same went for an unarmed, and unknown, person closing the distance to me.

"Stop!"

I yelled the command knowing that it would not be heeded. Less than a second later a lowered shoulder drove into my midsection and hands pummeled my face. Gloved hands. I fell backward, keeping a tight grip on my Springfield with one hand, the other trying to block the fists punching awkwardly at me. Off balance, I caromed off one side of the hallway and tumbled to the floor, the intruder's motion never stopping as she scrambled over me and skittered across the floor toward the front door.

She...

I was certain it was a woman now. The sound of a grunting breath being exhaled as we slammed to the hardwood convinced me of that, enough timbre in what I could hear to allow the distinction. I wondered for an instant as I rolled to get up and give chase if it could be someone from the town. A female teen, possibly, though the assumption had always been that any mischief was being carried out by boys. Doing so, though, only fed into a stereotype that had been disproven to me on many occasions. The 'fairer' sex could be just as badass as their more testosterone fueled brethren. My wife, who'd taken out a hulking Russian to save my life in the pit near Skagway, was as hard and as capable as any man I'd known. She'd taken a bullet aboard the *Groton Star* off the coast of Bandon, and crossed the wasteland to reach Cheyenne with Neil and me. And, she'd brought new life into this world.

The woman who'd just laid me out in my own home was made of the same stuff. That my bruised body could attest to with complete honesty.

By the time I was to me feet and starting toward the door she had thrown it open and sprinted out. Gusts whipped the screen door back and forth, slapping it against its frame and the front clapboards. I was out just after the intruder, catching a veiled glimpse of her running through the blizzard, backtracking down the side of my house. I could have gone back through the interior and tried to cut her off where the backdoor let out, but there was every chance she would just cut across the neighbor's back yard and still be ahead of me. I bolted off the front porch, my weapon held low in one hand, and chased the woman into the whiteout.

Five

She did cut across the neighbor's back yard, tramping fast through snow covered beds that Mrs. Traeger had said would be brimming with tomatoes and squash come summer and fall. I crossed the same space, building drifts slowing me, but also slowing the intruder. The distance between us stayed the same, about ten yards, as she weaved through more yards, down more driveways, aiming, I was certain, for the still dead woods a few blocks away.

For the second time that night, I was wrong about her intentions.

The fleeing intruder cut sharply to the left, around the back of a vacant house about mid-block, running directly into the wind, the icy snow scouring my cheeks as I squinted and followed. Another quick turn and she was now tracking up the side of the house, in essence doubling back.

What is she doing?

My silent wondering lasted only until I, too, made that turn, stopping after a few steps when I found myself facing the fat, suppressed end of an MP5 and the masked man who wielded it.

"Toss it," the man ordered me, just his dark eyes visible through the oval opening of his balaclava.

I knew what he wanted. The Springfield I held low and at ease, almost dangling in my right hand. It was my instrument of defense, or offense, depending on one's perspective. To the man blocking my way, it was that latter.

"Toss it."

His directive was spoken with calm force, words and tone cutting through the howl of the storm, softened by half in the lee of the adjacent house. He needn't disarm me to kill me. A simple squeeze of the trigger by his gloved finger would end me instantly. So might further refusal of his order.

I chose, at that moment, to acquiesce.

My right hand swung away from my body and let the pistol slip free. It sailed a few feet away, burying itself, I imagined, in a nearby drift. I wasn't looking so I could only guess. My attention remained on the man with the suppressed submachinegun pointed at my face.

The woman I'd chased was nowhere to be seen. She'd sprinted past the man, her backup, and disappeared into the storm. And, step by step, that was how my visual of him receded. He walked backward, slowly, never lowering his compact weapon, waves of white sweeping between us as he cleared the front edge of the houses to either side, the blizzard's full fury finally erasing him from the world before me.

I waited for a moment until I was certain the intruder's partner was gone, then I dug my Springfield from the snow and hurried back through the blinding snow to my house.

Six

"Do you think it was Olin?"

Martin's question was the obvious one to pose. Tyler Olin, after murdering my friend, had slipped away. There'd been no trace of him since his final phone call to me from one of the abandoned bunkers. A call in which I'd promised to end him should our paths ever cross again.

"It wasn't him," I said.

Perhaps it was that threat that had kept him from reappearing, though I had doubts as to whether he'd heard my statement of vengeance. When the bunker had been checked, all that was found was the field phone, out of its cradle, lying on the table. He'd simply set it down and disappeared.

Schiavo and Lorenzen came back into the living room from their brief search of the rest of the house. Hart, Westin, and Enderson, the remainder of the garrison, were out in the still raging storm, attempting to track down the intruder I'd scared off, as well as the man who'd been waiting to cover any retreat.

Though, I had to remind myself, the latter didn't seem at all afraid when I was staring past the muzzle of his weapon at him.

"I can't see anything obvious that he took," Lorenzen said. "Maybe later you can give the place a once over to see if you notice anything gone."

Later...

That would be a time when I was no longer alone in the house. In our house.

"Elaine is gonna be worried that I'm—"

Schiavo didn't give me a chance to finish voicing my worry.

"I called Grace and asked her to let Elaine know you had to help us with a situation."

I knew my wife. She would buy that explanation for about three seconds before starting to demand a real answer from Grace, and Genesee, and anyone else in earshot. It was possible that the presence our newborn daughter would mellow her reaction some, but, my limited understanding of genetics notwithstanding, it was just as likely that Hope would take after her mother and join in the protest with wails of disapproval.

"I have to get back there," I said.

"We'll get this place back together," Martin said. "I'll bolt a plywood patch over that broken pane in the door. That'll do until we can replace the glass."

Other than that, and a few drawers left hastily open, there was no sign that anyone had broken in. Not inside, at least.

"This wasn't some simple break-in," Corporal Mo Enderson said as he came through the front door, the wind howling for a second as Westin and Hart followed him in, the last trooper closing it against a stubborn gust. "You were targeted."

"How do you know that?" Martin pressed.

Westin stepped past his comrade, rifle slung and hands free to hold a pair of items—a radio and some folded piece of paper, water staining it from melting snow clinging to its surface.

"These were in the drifts just off your porch," Westin explained. "The one who ran from you must have dropped them."

It made sense I thought as I reached out and took the handheld radio from Westin. The click I'd heard was the transmit button being depressed, and the softened voice was the intruder warning their partner outside that they had a problem. I pressed the button myself to be certain, and the sound was identical.

"This is the kicker," Westin added, unfolding the paper so that all who'd gathered at my house after I'd called in the incident could see clearly what it was.

"A map," Martin said.

Westin nodded and passed it to his captain. Schiavo examined it for a moment, then passed it to me as I gave the radio back to the garrison's com expert.

"It's this entire block," Schiavo said as I studied the simple but accurate sketch of the neighborhood.

"With everyone's house labeled," Martin added, looking on from where he stood next to me. "Yours is circled, Fletch."

I nodded, marveling quietly, and with worry, at what I held in my hands. Names were penned neatly next to each structure. The road was marked. It was not to perfect scale, but it didn't need to be. Its purpose, apparently, was to guide the intruder and her partner to the house I shared with my wife, and soon our daughter.

Enderson was right—I was targeted.

"This could be the same crew who's hit the other houses," Enderson suggested.

"A few chickens have disappeared, too," Lorenzen reminded everyone. "No way to be sure, but the workers tending the coops have also said that the numbers of eggs have seemed light more than a few times."

What I, and others in the town, had experienced was beginning to seem like part of an organized effort. One that, until tonight, had been staged with covert skill.

"This isn't one of us doing this," Martin said, his statement directed to his wife. "It's outsiders."

Schiavo nodded, a tiredness in the affirmative gesture. We'd fought, and struggled, and fought again. Against remnants of a Cold War era adversary, and against rogue elements of our own government and its forces. People were weary of conflict. I was, as well. But now we were, once again, facing a challenge to our security, and our safety, from an unknown group which had penetrated our borders.

"There's more," Westin said, adjusting the frequency dial on the radio. "They have us dialed in."

"What do you mean?" Schiavo pressed.

Westin nodded to Hart and the medic took his own radio and briefly keyed the transmit button. A burst of static sounded from the captured radio.

"They've been listening to us," Westin said.

I looked to Schiavo, a broader understanding of what had occurred settling in.

"They knew I wouldn't be here," I said. "Or shouldn't be here."

I'd been standing with Schiavo on the beach when the call came summoning me to the hospital where Elaine had been taken. If there was a more certain indication than childbirth that our house would be at least temporarily vacant, I didn't know of it.

"It looks that way," Schiavo said, shifting her attention to Martin. "We need to know if any of the other people who've had break-ins had their absence announced on the radio."

Martin gave a quick, silent nod. His wife was turning to him again, tasking him with gathering information that she, and the Defense Council, would need to take appropriate action in this matter. With the Unified Government forces surrounding Bandon, Martin had worked tirelessly, and in the shadows, to uncover the infiltrator we had in our midst. He'd succeeded then, in a difficult task with dire consequences. The stakes, at the moment, seemed much lower here, but I knew the man who'd led Bandon through its worst times would treat what needed to be done with the utmost seriousness, and do so in confidence.

"This could just be the two Fletch ran into," Lorenzen suggested.

"That would make sense," Enderson agreed. "They went out of their way to not hurt Fletch."

"Says the man who didn't have a gun pointed at his face," I said.

"You know what he means," Schiavo said, standing up for her trooper.

I did. The moment was still raw, and, I had to admit, I was rattled by it. My home, where my wife slept, and where my daughter soon would, had been violated. Nothing troubled me more than the fear that I couldn't protect the ones I loved.

"If they'd shot you, Fletch, we'd be out hunting them down," Lorenzen said, giving voice to the reality we all understood. "If you're two, three, four people, you don't want some posse on your tail."

"That's how I would play it," I said, validating what seemed to be the consensus. "So, what do we do?"

Schiavo thought on that for a moment. Some action would have to be taken, beyond just verifying that the same individuals had been responsible for the other break-ins.

"I need to talk to the mayor," Schiavo said, looking to me. "You okay with all this, Fletch?"

I gave the space a look. I knew by the time I reached the hospital, Martin would already be working to patch the broken window. When we brought our daughter home in a day or two, almost no physical sign would remain that anything out of the ordinary had happened.

But I would know. And I would not be able to forget.

Seven

Two days after the break-in we brought our daughter home with the earth shimmering white under a perfect blue morning sky. Aside from Mrs. Traeger beaming at our bundled newborn from where she'd waited at the curb, and a quick welcome from our down-the-street neighbor, Dave Arndt, we were alone.

"This feels weird," Elaine said as we stood over Hope, watching her sleep in her crib. "Really weird."

"It kinda does," I agreed.

In the old world I'd listened to married friends describe the arrival of their firstborns in similar terms. From the bustle of activity surrounding the birth, to the constant presence of medical professionals ready to assist, the time before returning home with the new addition to the family felt almost normal. There was support. Advice. Company.

Then, you were alone.

It was not that we could not have had someone, or more than someone, there to help us with Hope. Any one of a dozen or more people would have dropped everything to do whatever it was we wanted, or needed. But, as many new parents did, we felt the desire to have some family time as we came home for the first time as a family.

"What do we do?" Elaine asked.

"I think this is what we do."

Standing in the dim room, just a nightlight glowing from a plug near the door, I imagined that I could stand there all night, just staring. Taking in every inch of our daughter, her body swaddled snugly, head topped by a pink cap, wisps of dark hair poking free.

"It's cliché to say she's perfect, isn't it?"

"It is," I told my wife. "But she is."

I looked to the woman who'd brought this miracle into the world, expecting to see her smiling sweetly at our child. She was smiling, but there was also a sheen of tears on her eyes, and a hint of something that did not seem to fit the moment—sadness.

"What's wrong?"

Elaine never looked at me as she spoke, her gaze fixed wholly on our daughter.

"So many people have died. Just so, so many. And here we are, and here she is. Why are we the lucky ones? Why?"

We were lucky, I knew. But there was more to our survival than fortune smiling on us.

"We fought for this," I reminded her. "We fought for her. I don't know if that means that we deserve to be alive, to be here, but I know it means we've earned this shot to go on. And to give her a shot at a future."

Now Elaine looked to me. She'd brightened a bit, maybe by a degree or two, but some sadness lingered.

"Fifty eight," she said, explaining after a moment. "That's how many bodies they pulled from the ocean."

I'd almost forgotten about the San Diego survivor colony, which had, apparently, perished in a storm at sea while attempting to reach us. To reach safety. Presumably from the Unified Government forces who'd taken Yuma and moved on to the coastal city at the extreme southern edge of California.

"Genesee was talking to Grace last night in the hall outside my room," she said. "I heard him tell her about all the bodies. All the..."

I reached out and pulled her into a gentle hug, stroking the back of her head, her hair cool and smooth against my hand.

"They're being buried today," Elaine reminded me. "At one."

I remembered. A crew had worked through the night to prepare graves in an unused section of the town cemetery, pushing past the boundaries of that property to a fallow field that had been considered for use as an orchard in the next planting season. Now it would be the final resting place for those the ocean had given up, the remainder of their friends and loved ones lost at sea.

"You know most of the town will be there," Elaine said, easing half out of our embrace to look me in the eye. "You should go. For both of us."

I shook my head. Fifteen feet from where we stood was the temporarily patched window where the intruders had reached through and unlocked the back door. At least one of them had pawed around our house, likely even the room in which we stood. The room where our daughter now slept. How was I supposed to leave Elaine and Hope alone, knowing that had happened?

"Eric..."

"I don't care if it's illogical that they'd come back. I'm not leaving you here."

Elaine stepped fully back from me, not in anger, but with full assurance about herself.

"Are you playing the 'man' card again?"

Her challenge was not born of nothing. I'd tried to shield her from danger in the past, only to have her rebel against what she must have thought was over protectiveness. Some chivalrous attempt to keep her from harm. She wasn't wrong in that belief.

But I'd been wrong in my belief that she *needed* me to protect her. Still, that didn't negate my desire to do be there for her. And now for our daughter as well.

"Elaine..."

"Listen, I want you here with me. With us. I want that more than anything. But, in case you haven't noticed, you're kind of a big part of this town now."

"I'm just—"

"No, you're not just anything."

Her counter to me was forceful enough that our daughter stirred at the sudden sound. Elaine took me gently by the elbow and took me into the hall with her.

"People see you as a leader, Eric. Not some elected or appointed figurehead, but a real, honest to goodness man who steps up and does what's necessary. What's right. And the right thing to do today is to go to the service. That's what the man I fell in love with would do."

I hated, absolutely hated it when she was right beyond argument. That she was complimenting me at the same time made it even harder to defy. But I was also touched by the faith she was exhibiting toward me. By the words that might seem just proxy for what others apparently saw in me, but were heartfelt on her part as well.

"You make it impossible for me not to love you," I said.

"Good," she said.

She stepped close and planted a soft kiss on my lips. A few feet away our daughter cooed softly. We both looked. Looked and held each other and watched our Hope, lying in her crib, peaceful and sweet. For the moment, this was all I needed. All I could have hoped for.

That such a state of bliss would last, I wanted to believe. I wanted so much to believe.

Eight

Over five hundred people attended the service in the cemetery, crowding between the headstones of old graves, thick layer of snow atop grass browned for the season. There was no lowering of caskets, as there was no wood to spare for making so many on such a short notice. Instead, by the time the first people arrived to pay their respects, the departed had already been placed in rectangular holes cut eight feet into the earth by one of the town's two working backhoes. Words were spoken by Reverend Harold Morris. It was twenty minutes total in the chill of the wintry afternoon air.

And that was it.

People wandered away, families and friends and neighbors grouped and chatting, some sharing stories of their brief interactions with members of the San Diego survivor colony that had taken place during times of darkness and elation in Skagway. Snippets of lives recounted. Brief recollections. That's all that was left of their lives, most buried nameless, only a few bearing identification on their person that would allow some marker to be crafted with any true specificity.

"It's important that we did this."

I looked to my right, to the familiar voice. Grace smiled at me, Brandon bundled and asleep on her shoulder.

"So many have died with no remembrance," she said.

"You sound like Elaine."

"Thank you," Grace said, taking my simple statement of fact as the compliment it was.

"Where's Krista?"

Grace gestured with a nod. Just beyond, her daughter was jogging ahead of those leaving the cemetery, obvious haste about her.

"She's in a heck of a hurry," I said, and Grace smiled at her daughter just before she disappeared beyond the entrance to the cemetery.

"It's almost two," Grace said. "She's late."

I puzzled at what she'd said.

"The broadcast," Grace reminded me.

"Right."

Our beacon. That's how I thought of the daily broadcast, transmitted at precisely one in the afternoon, every single day for the past two months since the Defense Council had authorized the effort to bring any still alive into our community. To grow our population. Krista had taken on the responsibility, with the blessing of the garrison's com expert, Westin, who I was certain was pleased to be freed of the rather mundane task. Krista had embraced that aspect of her time at Micah's transmitter, just as she'd done at my Montana refuge while attempting to connect with Eagle One.

"She loves being useful," Grace told me.

"Just imagine her at twenty," I said. "She'll be running this town."

Grace nodded, though it wasn't a wholly joyful expression of agreement.

"She won't know a real childhood," Grace said.

That was true in many respects. But the world was what it was. And we were doing our best to make what rose from the ashes a better place, not just a flawed recreation of the flawed original.

"She's a pioneer," I told Grace. "When we're bones in the ground, she'll be able to look back and know how far we came. That may not be the way it should have been, but, it's not a bad thing."

Grace accepted my honest, if hopeful, appraisal with a nod.

"You should probably get home to that new baby," Grace said.

"That's the plan."

I leaned in and gave my friend's widow a peck on the cheek, and planted another on the beanie-covered head of their son, dead to the world on her shoulder. Soon Brandon would move beyond toddling. He would walk. Run. Fall. Get up. He would have a childhood the same as my Hope would.

"You should bring the kids by," I said. "Elaine would love the company."

Grace nodded and grinned, knowing and doubt in the gesture.

"Yeah, I think you're gonna need a few days to acclimate," she said. "Trust me."

She reached out with her free hand and put a palm against my cheek, then tapped it playfully before turning and following the tail end of the procession of townspeople out of the cemetery, leaving me alone.

But as I began walking toward the exit, I realized I was not the last one present in the place where the dead rested for eternity. A dozen yards away, near a bare pear tree, its limbs stripped of their leaves by the season, a man stood. A good man.

"Doc..."

Everett Allen, man of medicine, mayor of our town, turned toward me as I approached. He managed a smile, then once again faced the headstone that marked the grave of his wife.

"How are you, Fletch?"

"I'm a father," I told him. "That makes me ecstatic and terrified."

The man I would always think of as Doc, despite his political title, gave a light chuckle and turned back to the slab of chiseled stone bearing the name Carol Allen. A pair of artists, more used to working with clay and paints in the world as it was, came together to craft the headstone for the man, and his late wife, who were respected by all. He stood on the wintry carpet and reached a bare hand to brush snow from the top of the marker.

"I just wanted to spend a little time with my girl after the service," he said.

I felt a warm bulge build in my throat, emotion rising at the simple display of love the man had for the woman that was no longer at his side. Decades of marriage, of companionship, had forged a bond that separation by death could not break. It was a lovely, heartbreaking thing to bear witness to.

"This tree's going to be lovely once spring comes," I said.

He finished clearing the top of his wife's stone and looked to the nearby pear tree, gangly, barren limbs seeming pained and lifeless. But within there was vigor just waiting for the slumber to pass.

"It'll be nice shade," he said. "I was thinking about bringing a folding chair up here with me once it warms up. On occasion. Then I can sit and have a nice talk with her."

"That sounds nice," I told the doc.

He considered my affirmation for a moment, then his smile grew a bit, and he set a knowing gaze upon me.

"It sounds like an old man who doesn't know what to do with himself now that half of who he was is gone."

"Doc..."

He waved off my apologetic concern.

"Fletch, that's just the way I grieve. I imagined most folks my age do the same when they lose the love of their life."

Words were all I had to offer, and words were inadequate. At least to me they were.

"You should come by and see Hope," I said, ignoring Grace's advice to embrace the 'we' time that Elaine and I would have with our daughter. "She's kind of adorable."

"I imagine she's just that and a fair measure more. I'll pay a visit in a few days after you and Elaine get used to not being a duo anymore."

I nodded and took in the feel of the winter's day. It was cold but not bone chilling. Not like Montana winters could be. This was an anomaly. A freak blizzard that blanketed and battered the coast. Were there news stations still reporting, I imagine it would have been a major story. A storm of suitably biblical proportions—or at least the news copy would read as such. So much of the old world that had been hyped in both good times and bad now seemed so...mundane. The world was real now. What we saw and felt and experienced had little, if any, filters. Truths were easier to identify.

At least in the case of Doctor Everett Allen. He was putting on a brave face. Carrying on. Surviving.

But this act of survival, compared to what he'd gone through to weather the blight and the collapse of civilization, was taking a greater toll. I could see that in him. In the slackness of his shoulders. In his weary smile. His almost listless gaze.

The truth I knew at this moment was that I was worried about him.

"Do come by, Doc," I said. "Please."

He reached out and shook my hand, but said no more. I left him, and when I looked back just before passing through the open cemetery gates I could see him, one hand planted on his wife's headstone, leaning against it, his gaze cast upward, to the blue heavens above.

Nine

We were making progress and moving backward at the same time.

Six women were expecting, and the town's sewage had begun to flow into the Coquille River, untreated. The grazing fields had greened enough through spring and summer to support our livestock without requiring the pulp processor, and a pair of cows had escaped their fenced pasture and were struck and killed by a military truck hauling barrels of diesel from the refining plant. Sapling spruce and fir trees had been planted and were growing, but one of the bee colonies brought in on the *Rushmore*'s first visit to Bandon had swarmed and headed off, perhaps confused by the scent of dead foliage persistent in the air.

And, yet again, we'd been reminded that we were not alone. The pilfering, which had initially been blamed on local youth, was discovered to be the act of outsiders. How many was not known. Possibly it was just the two I'd encountered, a man and a woman. A couple who'd survived and were scavenging in carefully planned intrusions. Talk amongst the members of the Defense Council had turned to the question if the town needed to increase its readiness once more, as it had when the Unified Government forces surrounded us on three sides. Not to that level of preparation for armed conflict, but sufficient to have some chance of stopping the thieves before one of our own was hurt. Or worse.

But the most exciting thing to happen, in terms of reestablishing humanity's foothold on a brighter future, had nothing to do with any efforts we'd undertaken. Or with any vigor we applied to our own defense. It came by chance, with Dave Arndt walking near the beach one morning, staring absently out to the Pacific. Twenty minutes later, after a giddily frantic call from him over the radio, a good half the town was crammed onto a bluff, some with binoculars, though Dave had assured us that none would be necessary.

"Just keep looking," he told us.

Schiavo and Martin stood with me, Sergeant Lorenzen and Specialist Hart on the far side of the crowd, every eye fixed on the ocean, gazes sweeping the rolling waters beyond the towering rocks. Once again I hadn't wanted to come when the phone rang at our house, and once again Elaine reminded me of the status I'd achieved in the town, telling me it would raise questions if I was absent from a potentially important event. That was how Martin had relayed the information to me, saying that Dave assured that what we would see would 'shake the earth'. In light of the spate of temblors we'd experienced, his choice of words was probably not appropriate. More telling, though, was his refusal to tell anyone what he saw, insisting that it had to be seen so that its full effect could be experienced.

"I have a baby at home I could be gawking at," I said.

A week it had been since our daughter arrived. Seven days of sleepless nights and restless days. And I'd loved every minute of it. Every second with the being which I had no concept how much I could love.

"If Dave Arndt says we need to see something," Martin told me.

"I know," I agreed.

Dave was as solid a citizen as they came. There had to be a compelling reason for him to be as cagy as he was being.

A few seconds after I had that thought, the reason became abundantly clear in a shower of spray a few hundred yards off the beach.

"Holy..."

Schiavo's truncated reaction was almost lost amongst the gasps and joyful curses rolling through the crowd.

"Was that a..."

Martin, too, seemed stunned to the point of near silence by what we'd just seen.

"Yes," Dave said. "That's a whale."

Despite the promise that we wouldn't need binoculars to see what would happen, an assurance that had been spot on, Schiavo raised those that she'd brought along and zeroed in on the continuing event, more blasts from the creature's blowhole jetting upward beyond the light surf.

"This isn't possible," I said with obvious uncertainty. "Is it?"

"Apparently we're not the only survivors," Martin said.

"Many species of whales subsist on the tiniest organisms in the ocean," Dave Arndt said. "A lot of those live off of decaying matter. Which, one can assume, has been plentiful in everywhere after in the wake of the blight."

"Even hundreds of feet under the sea?" Schiavo asked, lowering the binoculars as she laid a doubting gaze on the man.

"Hey, college was a long time ago," Dave said. "And I took Marine Biology because I needed a science course, not because I expected to need it to understand this. But that's what I remember."

Schiavo thought on that for a moment, then flashed Dave a smile.

"Fair enough," she said, turning to Martin and me next. "If something that big survived..."

"Maybe there's hope for a fishing fleet somewhere down the road," Martin surmised.

Bandon had been a fishing village at one time, and up until the blight struck a small number of boats made their way past the lighthouse on a near daily basis to seek their bounty from the ocean. I'd been told this by more than one local who'd known the joy of fresh fish purchased right off the dock, and I wanted to think that, someday, I'd be able to experience the same with Elaine and Hope.

That, though, was a day which might be far off. Right now it was enough to see what we were, and to realize how buoying it was to everyone's spirits. That collective joy was plain in the crowd that had come to witness proof that nature was more resilient than we'd given it credit for.

But the numbers that I saw behind me, staring with glee out to the ocean, did not represent all who lived in Bandon. Nor all who I'd expected would be present. A very distinct group of residents was not in attendance. Their absence, I thought, could be nothing other than purposeful.

And that purpose was made plain to me less than twenty-four hours later after a knock on my door.

Ten

They didn't approach Mayor Allen, or Captain Schiavo. Or even her husband, Martin, who'd led Bandon through the worst of times to a more prosperous now.

They chose me to share that they wanted to leave.

"We want to start fresh somewhere," Mike DeSantis said as we stood in the shelter of my porch, a light rain falling beyond. "It's time, Fletch."

The man, who'd just turned forty, was not a Bandon local. He'd come to the isolated town a few months before I'd arrived. Originally from Seattle, he knew that there was no returning to that city, if there was anything left of it to go home to. Besides being overrun by the drug-crazed hordes soon after the blight ravaged our civilization, it was to be expected that every manner of human caused disaster had plagued the once shining city. Fires. Vandalism. Contamination. Destruction.

"Is there any more reason than what you've said?" I asked.

Mike looked to those who'd accompanied him to my house—Nick Withers and Rebecca Vance. Neither appeared to be keen on elaborating any more than what their spokesman had already offered. But what they were suggesting, or even planning, I felt deserved at least some measure of explanation.

"This isn't a prison," I said. "No one is going to force anyone to stay where they don't want to be. But a lot of people have sacrificed, have given everything there is to give, so that you all can stand here right now and freely say you want to turn your back on that."

"It's not like that, Fletch," Nick said.

Nick and I had come through a firefight in the woods nearly a year ago. He'd experienced first-hand what facing death was.

"Fletch, people weren't happy with the captain during the siege," Mike said. "A good number of people. Dozens."

To be certain, Captain Angela Schiavo had made some tricky decisions during the time our town was encircled by the Unified Government forces, and I'd warned her that some would be resistant to her desire to collect a portion of the residents' personal ammunition stores. But had the reaction to that, or to something else, risen to the level that some of our friends, our neighbors, now wanted to flee the community beginning to rise from the ashes of the blight?

"We lost more than half our ammo," Rebecca reminded me. "Half, Fletch."

The woman spoke to me with an AK strapped across her back

"And what is with this so-called Defense Council?" Rebecca challenged. "Defense against what?"

"The unknown," I answered, with complete honesty.

"It sounds authoritarian," Mike said.

It was clear they held strong feelings about the concerns they were airing. I had to remind myself that, even if I did not agree with their beliefs and any conclusions they were drawing, I had to attempt to be understanding. These were good people, I knew. Good people who were drifting away from what Bandon was, and what it was becoming.

"And now there's talk about bringing the checkpoints back," Nick said.

"We've had intruders," I reminded them. "You know that. We have to be on guard."

"Right," Rebecca said, her sarcasm plain. "First it was local kids doing the robberies. Now it's some big scary unknown group of people. This is classic manipulation by the government, Fletch. You know that. You saw it when the blight first hit. Distract the people from what's really happening. Stage events."

I'd seen plenty, but I hadn't seen anything staged. Not the shooting of the driver at the checkpoint near Arlee, nor the downing of the passenger jet by an Air Force fighter played over and over on the TV news. Maybe Rebecca had seen things which I hadn't been privy to. Or maybe she was letting old fears and beliefs inform her view of the present.

"It's probably just a few people, Rebecca," I told her. "We're just being cautious. There's no army out there again."

"So you say."

I wasn't getting through to her. In fact, I wasn't sure I should even bother trying. It was plain to me that they'd come here with their mind made up. They'd thought this through, agreed on a course of action, and taken the first steps to make that happen.

"Fletch," Mike began, "the bottom line is that a group of us wants to settle somewhere else. To have more control over how we do things."

"And don't do things," Rebecca added, some fire still in her.

Nick reached into an old bag slung from one shoulder and retrieved something. It was small and wrapped with plain brown paper, but a bright pink ribbon circled it, a frilly bow topping the obvious present.

"We brought this for Hope," Nick said, handing the gift over.

I took it and eyed the offering.

"We found it in Remote," Mike said. "We've run several scavenging patrols there and past that, almost to Camas Valley."

Remote, a town that fit its name. If one could call the collection of houses and an old, small store a town. Forty plus miles inland, it was near the limits of where our regular patrols had penetrated inland seeking to gather supplies that still existed across the landscape—clothing, weapons, ammunition, tools, batteries. The latter was the most crucial, as the supplies of the once ubiquitous items used to power flashlights and some portable radios was dwindling. As it was, we had no one with the skills in chemistry to recreate the necessity, though attempts had been made, all unsuccessful, and some outright dangerous. Minor explosions had convinced those involved to suspend their efforts until more brain power could be brought to the table. Our broadcasts to any survivors was crucial to that, and to other aspects of our recovery. Beckoning those who'd weathered the blight to join us would serve to bring new, maybe needed skills into our numbers.

And now, those numbers, it appeared, would be decreasing before we'd get any response to our beacon. No fresh influx of souls who'd managed to survive what had almost been the end of the world had yet materialized, to our collective frustration.

"That's where we want to settle, Fletch," Mike said. "In Remote."

"Remote," I parroted. "Remote?"

"We know it's not much," Nick said.

"It's actually perfect," Rebecca interjected. "And it would be ours. All ours."

I looked between the three residents. The three friends. Neighbors. Two of those things were going to change if they went through with their plan to leave. I didn't want our friendship, however tenuous it might be on an individual basis, to be ended by this. By any of this.

"You want me to let the Council know about this," I said, lifting the present a bit as I spoke. "You didn't just come bearing gifts and news, right?"

"We have some demands—"

"Requests," Mike said, cutting Rebecca off. "Requests."

"Fletch, you're right," Nick said. "We did come to you to act as a sort of...intermediary. The people on the Council listen to you. They trust you."

People see you as a leader...

Elaine had told me that. I'd also felt that, but was never comfortable with people putting an inordinate amount of trust in me.

Apparently, though, that was exactly what was happening just beyond the front door of my house. Behind the trio who'd come to me, the light rain had lessened further, just a wispy mist settling upon the yard, and the street. And upon the town they wanted to leave.

And I was to be their messenger.

"I'm listening," I said.

Eleven

"How many?"

Mayor Allen waited for an answer as Schiavo and Martin looked on.

"Forty," I said.

"Forty?" Martin asked, surprised by the number. "*Forty* people want to leave?"

I nodded. Martin rose from his seat at the conference table in the Town Hall, this gathering of the Defense Council off to a sobering start. He walked to the window and looked out. From his vantage, not much of the town could be seen. But it was out there. They were out there. The people he'd helped shepherd through the worst of the blight. He'd given up the mantle of leadership, but the responsibility for Bandon's wellbeing was a feeling he could not shed.

"Forty," he repeated, his breath briefly fogging the window and blotting the world outside from view.

"Martin..."

The man turned and looked to me.

"This isn't necessarily a bad thing," I told him.

"There is strength in numbers, Fletch," he said.

"And keeping all our eggs in one basket isn't always the wisest strategy," I countered.

In that instant, right after I spoke, Mayor Allen and Captain Schiavo exchanged a look. What I'd just stated, so simple a concept, immediately had meaning that none of us had considered. Until now.

"We have to face the reality that in Bandon, we only have Bandon," I said. "A new settlement would expand our footprint. No different than the planting we have set for spring."

In a few months, with the weather right, teams would set out from town to begin planting sapling trees which had been germinating in greenhouses. Scattered throughout the once green forests, set to sprout in clearings where mighty pines and firs had once towered, this new growth would, we hoped, begin the regeneration of the landscape.

If new homesteads beyond our borders could also sprout, and flourish, then we, too, would be fulfilling our destiny. To grow. Expand. Thrive.

"Also, with settlements, we have outposts," I continued. "Each could serve as a warning of anything like the approach of the Unified Government forces."

"And if this group leaves, Fletch, what then?" Mayor Allen asked, a true concern in his voice. "Next week another forty go. Then fifty. Maybe ten the next week."

"And pretty soon we're not much of a town anymore," Schiavo said.

I knew there'd be resistance. Even I wanted the would-be settlers to stay. But there was a natural order to this that it had taken me a few hours to grasp. I could only hope that those with me would do so much more quickly.

"We want to grow," I said. "But maybe we should be more concerned about growing the species. Because that will be much easier with diverse groupings. Our species can weather illness, disasters, attacks much better if we are not all in the same physical location."

"Maybe," Martin said. "But that's not behind this. They just don't care for the leadership."

I'd shared their sense of discontent with some decisions that were made, particularly those actions taken by Schiavo in the heat of out fight with the Unified Government forces. Martin, I thought, was mostly reacting as a former leader of Bandon. But I also sensed that there was a measure of animus that came from his wife being the source of such scorn.

"The bottom line is, they're leaving," I said. "And we need to figure out how we can support them."

Mayor Allen sat back in his chair, considering what I'd just said. Martin took the seat next to his wife and could only shake his head.

"There are things they would like in order to make this go smoothly," I told the Council.

"Things they want," Martin repeated. "That's rich."

Schiavo gave her husband a sideways look, then faced me again.

"What sort of things?" she asked.

"A small supply of livestock once they are settled in," I shared. "Medical care when necessary. Those are the major items. Everything else is supply oriented."

Schiavo looked to Mayor Allen, each seeming to weigh the possibilities of what I'd told them. That mere act of entertaining what was being proposed visibly agitated Martin. He stood again, eyeing each of us, a joyless chuckle slipping past his lips.

"Are you all forgetting we're in the middle of trying to figure out who's penetrating our security?" he challenged us. "And you want to allow some permanent foray beyond our protection?"

"Martin," Schiavo began, "what we want isn't really relevant. What matters is what they want."

"I don't see how we can prevent anyone from striking out on their own," Mayor Allen agreed.

For a moment, Martin just stood there, seething within, controlling his reaction as best he could. Then, with a breath that came almost involuntarily, he closed his eyes briefly and nodded.

"I know," he said, leaning against the window sill. "I know."

I'd fulfilled my duty to bring this information to the Council. I'd acted as intermediary to see that the issue was handled smoothly. My part in this was done.

Except it wasn't.

"There is a problem, however," I said. "I've been to Remote on several scouting trips. It's not ready to be inhabited. There could be structural issues with some of the houses, and the bridges along the highway need to be checked."

"Several years of runoff and battering by dead trees that have fallen into the river," Mayor Allen said, reading exactly the concern I was alluding to.

"Do they know this?" Schiavo asked.

"They believe they can handle any repairs," I told her. "But that may be wishful thinking."

"They're going to need more support than a few goats and doctor visits," Martin said.

Schiavo processed the opinion I had shared, mulling that, and more, for a moment before addressing the town's elected leader.

"This should be a two way street. If we provide for their needs, something should flow our way."

"An agreement," the mayor said.

"A treaty," Schiavo clarified. "Something formal."

"Dear God," Martin said. "We're not the U.N."

"No," Schiavo mostly agreed. "But we might need to start acting more official at some point. This won't be the first group that wants to plant a flag somewhere else."

"On that note," I began, "there is one condition I told them was non-negotiable."

"What is that, Fletch?" Mayor Allen asked.

"I told them that they may be leaving Bandon, but they are not leaving the country. They're still Americans."

"And if they hadn't agreed, we wouldn't be having this meeting," Martin said.

I nodded. It might have been presumptuous on my part to insert some condition before the town's leadership had a chance to weigh in, but, to be honest, I didn't care. Without that stipulation, I would not be giving them the time of day. To my pleasure, their reaction had been more than acceptable.

"They said they'd fly the flag proudly," I told the Council, then took the opportunity to stand and slide my chair against the table. "Now, if it's not a problem, I'm going to let you all discuss any more issues related to this so I can go home and be with my family."

There were no objections, and I left the conference room, heading to the pickup truck I'd been allowed to use by the town. I was in the driver's seat and starting the engine when I realized I'd been followed from the Town Hall. The driver's window lowered easily at the touch of a button.

"Martin..."

He approached the open window and stood close.

"I wasn't doubting you in there," he said.

"I know this town means a lot to you. And the people."

But he shook his head at that fact I'd just stated.

"It's not that, Fletch. It's..."

"Martin, what is it?"

He hesitated just an instant, like one might before ripping of an adhesive bandage.

"I checked out all the other people who'd had break-ins," Martin told me, confirming what I'd already known he was doing. "None had any mention of their absence from their houses transmitted on the radio. Whoever broke in had to just see them leave."

"Crimes of opportunity," I said.

"I don't think so," Martin told me.

"I don't understand."

Martin stepped closer and made sure no one was in earshot before explaining.

"Fletch, your house was marked on a map. The intruders had a radio and would have heard you were at the hospital. You and Elaine."

"We know that, Martin."

"That was careful planning," he said. "So why weren't the others? There was no pattern to those houses being empty at the time the intruders hit. One was only empty because Christine Polk went across the street to sit on her friend's porch and watch the sunset. That's spur of the moment, Fletch. Completely unpredictable. You don't need a map and a radio to pull off that burglary."

He was right. But I still didn't know where he was going with the line of reason.

"Where are you saying, Martin?"

"What if the other break-ins were diversions?" the man asked and suggested in the same breath. "Corporal Enderson said you were targeted when they found that map and radio. Maybe he was more right that he knew."

I processed what the man had offered. The idea of being targeted was, oddly, not an alien possibility to me. I'd been snatched from a getaway with Elaine and left in the middle of nowhere. That, though, had been done at the behest of Neil in an effort to protect me, and to save the town we'd thought he'd abandoned. But this...

"These were strangers, Martin."

"So was Olin."

His reminder was true, but, still, a swing and a miss as I saw it.

"All this might mean is that they didn't drop their radio and maps at the other houses because they weren't interrupted," I told him.

"That's always a possibility," he said, with no conviction at all in the words he'd just spoken. "But so is my scenario."

To that I nodded, equally as unconvinced in his theory as he was in mine.

"Be careful, Fletch," he said.

He backed away from the truck and headed back into the Town Hall, having spoken his mind. I had no reason to doubt the sincerity of his belief, nor the man himself. But, in a way, I wondered if the recent events and indications of outsiders in our midst was resetting his manner of operation to one that was too defensive. We'd won the battle against the Unified Government. Martin, though, seemed to still be wary. To still be fighting.

I couldn't be too harsh on him, though. He'd lost a son, and then an unborn child. Loss was ingrained in what he'd known of this new world. That he was fearful for me, I could only take as an expression of caring.

But I had to live. Had to return to the place where my life, and its new chapter, were already playing out.

Twelve

I was alone in bed when I heard the sound.

It was well past midnight, I instinctively knew, and a quick glance at the bedside clock confirmed my estimation—twelve after two in the morning.

Through the open bedroom door I could hear the rhythmic, muffled squeak of the rocker we'd placed in the nursery. Elaine was in there, feeding Hope, having just risen a few minutes earlier at the sound of our newborn fussing. But it was not that very expected sound that drew my attention.

Something was moving outside.

Be careful, Fletch...

Martin's unexpected admonition echoed in my thoughts right then. Perhaps I'd internalized the warning I'd mostly discounted, allowing it to creep up from my subconscious as I was drifting back to sleep. That might have made me jumpy. Susceptible to alarm.

I allowed that possibility until I heard the noise again.

It rose up from the space below the window outside. In another place and time I would have simply thought a raccoon was scavenging. Or a possum. But those creatures were gone. They had not survived in old burrows for years as some whales apparently had in the deepest waters of the Pacific. No, something else was out there.

Someone.

I slid my legs over the edge of the bed and into my boots. There was no time to lace them, nor to add any clothing over the sweats and long tee I had worn to bed. From the nightstand door I took my Springfield, and I slipped slowly around the bed to Elaine's side. From the identical piece of furniture there I retrieved my wife's Glock. At some point in the near future, until out daughter could be taught to respect and use such weapons, we would have to devise some form of safe storage that would still allow us easy access. This night, this very moment, validated the need for such quick retrieval of our arms.

A few soft steps carried me out of the room and across the hall to the nursery. The soft glow of the nightlight revealed my wife there, in the rocker, cradling our daughter as she breastfed her. So focused was Elaine, so connected, that she did not note my appearance in the doorway.

"Hey."

She looked now, the tired but content expression she'd worn changing instantly when she saw what I carried in each hand. I reached out and laid her 9mm pistol on the changing table to one side.

"Something outside," I said in a hushed tone.

She glanced at her pistol, then looked to me again.

"Call it in," she said.

"I'm just going to check it out," I said.

With a careful motion she removed our daughter from her breast and brought her sweatshirt down. The child remained quiet, having fed enough. Elaine laid her gently in the crib and took her weapon in hand.

"You're not going out there," she told me.

It was quite the role reversal, I thought.

"You know how you don't like that overprotective streak in me?"

"This is different," she said.

"Elaine..."

"I'm calling it—"

Her words were cut off by the sound of glass shattering, and something breaking inside, toward the front of the house, followed by a flash of orange light and a whoosh of hot air rolling down the hallway.

"Get the baby!"

I shouted the instruction as Elaine was already returning to the crib, holding our daughter against her chest with one hand, pistol in the other. She was a grizzly mama, prepared to fight to the death for her child.

So was I.

I brought my Springfield up and stepped back into the hallway as black smoke gushed past me. Through the acrid cloud I could see flames, hot and angry, boiling in the living room.

"Out the back!"

Elaine ran past me, into the hallway, speeding toward the back way into the kitchen. A quick dash past the stove would take us out back and to safety. I turned away from the advancing flame and followed my wife, turning into the kitchen where I expected to see her already at the back door.

But I did not see that. I did not see that at all.

Elaine stood frozen, holding Hope close, a rifle pointed at her face from a few feet away. A lever action rifle, the man wielding it lit up by the fire's flickering light.

"Olin..."

"Eric..."

My wife's plaintive voice, so impossibly small and frightened, cut me worse than any weapon. Her pistol hung limp in one hand at her side, fear that any motion on her part would cause the man, the murderer, to fire, putting the child she'd brought into the world in jeopardy. That was something she would not do.

"What are you doing?" I demanded, the heat of the growing blaze stinging the left side of my body.

"Eric..."

Her repetition of my name stoked a separate fire, one inside of me. I had to protect her. Had to do anything to keep her and our daughter safe.

"What do you want?!"

I screamed the demand at Olin, but he said nothing. Gave no answer. He just stood there, .30-30 aimed at my wife's head, but his hateful gaze fixed on me as items in the kitchen began to smolder. Licks of smoke rose from the edges of the cabinets, and from a set of plastic bowls on the counter.

"Eric!"

I could stand it no more. I brought my Springfield up and aimed past Elaine, drawing a bead on the bridge of Olin's nose. Still, he made no move, his jacket beginning to smoke, as was my wife's thick sweatshirt. The inferno swirled into the kitchen, flames clawing toward us. Elaine screamed. Our daughter wailed. I heard myself cry out, cursing Olin as—

There was no sudden gasp or bolting upright in bed as I woke from the dream. From the nightmare. My eyes simply opened and it was over.

I rolled toward Elaine's side of the bed, but she was not there. My heart did not leap with fear. The very sweet sound from across the hallway soothed any worry that might have swept over me.

A moment later I stood in the doorway of our daughter's room, looking in at my wife singing a soft lullaby as she fed our daughter, a blanket knitted as a gift by a neighbor pulled around them against the slight chill inside.

"Couldn't sleep?" she asked, interrupting her quiet serenade when she saw me leaning on the doorjamb.

"Just heard you," I said, smiling.

It was odd, I thought, that I could so easily wipe the feelings of such a terrible, horrible dream from my waking thoughts so soon after experiencing them. I'd had disturbing dreams before, only rarely, including one of Neil gleefully throwing himself off a cliff. Elaine had woken me from that dream as I thrashed and cried out. So why hadn't I reacted in a similar way just now?

"I swore I'd never breast feed," Elaine told me, as if sharing some minor secret. "It was only going to be bottles and formula."

"When in Rome," I said.

She nodded and let her gaze settle on our daughter's blue, inquisitive eyes. Eyes that stared back into her mother's. I could have stayed focused on the very peaceful and touching moment before me, but I couldn't.

Olin...

The man had invaded my sleep in the most horrible way, and I'd slipped out of the dream without so much as a quickened heartbeat or a damp brow. How was that possible? I'd just subconsciously imagined myself standing by as a fire, set by the man who'd murdered Neil, consumed my family.

Maybe he didn't set it...

That bit of analysis came without warning, or request. I almost laughed at myself for attempting to decipher the why of the dream that vexed me now. If I'd been falling, wouldn't that have been easier? Those nightmares were about something unfinished, if I remembered correctly. But what did this dream suggest?

As I stared at my wife and daughter, at my perfect family that existed in an imperfect world, I began to come to some understanding. At least that was what my limited knowledge of the acts of the subconscious allowed me to theorize.

Abandonment.

That was my fear. That I would not be there for my family. That, if they were faced with some life threatening event, I would be absent. It would be as if I had to stand by and watch them suffer. Or perish.

And, at the same instant that I came to accept that interpretation, I knew exactly what was spawning it.

"The captain is going to ask me to go to Remote," I said.

Elaine looked easily up from our daughter, no shock or anxiousness about her. I'd shared with her what had transpired at the Defense Council. The birth of our daughter had kept her from attending the recent meetings, but she was still part of the group, and we'd all worked to keep her in the loop.

"I told them that the buildings out there might have issues."

"I remember," Elaine said.

One of the last scouting patrols she'd gone on, prior to dialing back her physical activity just two months before giving birth, was to Remote. On that scavenging foray she'd been with a group that did not include me, a reality that, at that point in her pregnancy, I found difficult to accept, much less embrace.

"She didn't say anything at the meeting, but..."

"But you have the experience to inspect what's there," Elaine said.

I nodded. My past life as a contractor, overseeing everything from the building of houses to commercial business parks, and the roads and infrastructure which connected them to civilization, made me uniquely qualified. If fact, there was not another person in Bandon who'd supervised such projects. We had carpenters and plumbers and electricians, but sizing up the suitability of Remote as a viable settlement would require a skillset of more depth and breadth. My skillset.

"I just don't want to be away from you and Hope," I said.

"Sometimes you'll have to be," Elaine reminded me. "Life won't stop just because of her."

Her...

I looked to our daughter. My wife was right—life could not stop. Nor slow down. It had to move forward. We, as a town, had to move forward. Expanding our footprint on the earth as the color green returned to the planet, and all the creatures that could thrive in a resurgent ecosystem, was imperative. Our future depended upon being successful in this first attempt at that.

More importantly, our daughter's future depended on it.

"So you're okay with it," I said. "It will be maybe a day. We'll be back before dark."

As she cradled our daughter against her breast, she reached out with her free hand. Toward me. I took it in mine and we each gave a little squeeze. A sign of reassurance. Of acceptance.

"I'm okay with anything you need to do," Elaine said.

In the worst of times, with the world teetering on the edge of destruction, I'd fallen in love with Elaine Morales. What I saw before me, and felt in my hand, validated that event. I was a lucky man. Maybe the luckiest.

Thirteen

Schiavo couldn't take her eyes off of Hope as she held her.

She'd stopped by just as Elaine was heading out for a walk, asking if she wanted to stay since there was something she needed to discuss. But my wife had waved off the invitation, signaling that she already knew what was about to transpire. I sensed that the captain knew this from their brief, very pleasant exchange.

There was small talk at first, and a request to hold our daughter, as she was now, sitting in the padded rocker near the fireplace, a pair of logs crackling in the hearth. Finally, after a few minutes, she looked up to where I stood, elbow on the mantle.

"Fletch, I need to ask a favor of you."

"Remote," I said.

"I need you to come with me and Specialist Hart," Schiavo said. "Tomorrow."

"Okay."

There was no need to delay sharing the decision I'd already made. I was only slightly less all right with it than Elaine, which, had she known that, would have soothed Schiavo. Her nearly formal visit to our home had been, I suspected, meant to assuage any fears my wife had about the mission.

The mission...

It was that, I supposed. We would be venturing beyond our borders, almost to the limits of where we'd sent patrols, just one of those previously going as far as Camas Valley, a larger town beyond Remote. We would be armed, of course, which was as prudent as it was within our own borders.

"You're the only person in town who can give an honest appraisal of the structures," Schiavo said. "I talked to Mike DeSantis about this, and he agreed to let the group know what we were doing."

"I'm sure Rebecca will find some fault with it," I told her.

"Civilizations without rebels turn stale," Schiavo said.

It was a simple defense of the woman who'd come at me with a fire in her belly. But it was also true.

"I know this will be hard," Schiavo said, gazing down at my daughter in her arms. "Leaving Elaine and...this."

This...

She was not choosing a vague descriptor of Hope for any purpose. Instead, I knew, she was making note of the fact that it was more than a child she was cradling. More than a gender. More than a species, even.

A life was sleeping sweetly in her embrace. A life which she might have known in her own home, with Martin. But that did not come to pass. A twist of fate, some unseen medical complication, or any of a number of factors had taken their child before the world could welcome it.

"You're a lucky man, Fletch."

Again, there was no contemplation necessary of the statement she'd made.

"I am."

The front door opened and I looked up to see Elaine. For just an instant she stood there, the chill of the season washing past her as she looked at us.

"I didn't tell you, Elaine," Schiavo began, "but you're looking wonderful."

"Thanks. The walk felt good."

Schiavo shifted in her chair, trying to stand. I stepped away from the mantle and eased our daughter from her so she could rise unencumbered. When she was up, her gaze met Elaine's, some silent understanding in the exchange.

"When do you leave?" Elaine asked.

"Tomorrow," Schiavo told her.

My wife smiled and gave a small nod of acceptance. Maybe of approval, as well.

"I'll see you about six," Schiavo told me. "We'll pick you up."

"I'll be ready."

She gave Elaine a quick hug and left us.

"She would have been a good mother," my wife said, watching Schiavo get behind the wheel of her Humvee and drive away.

I didn't disagree with her. In fact, I could see in the woman exactly what Elaine had. But I wondered if she would have chosen to remain in her position, and retain her rank, if she and Martin had welcomed a child into the world. It might have been a sexist reaction to the intense connection I'd witnessed between her and Hope, but there was also the reality of the matter. She'd been through a lot. More, in fact. Enough for several lifetimes in the few years since the blight had ravaged our world. That totality of experience, and struggle, and pain, made me think that, had Angela Schiavo, Captain, United States Army, welcomed a child, she very well might have considered her service complete and would have chosen to embrace fully the new adventure of motherhood.

At the very least, I knew that she would have adored having that choice to make.

"Do you want some hot chocolate?" Elaine asked.

A recent scavenging expedition testing the limits of our deserted northern neighbor, Coos Bay, had come across a tractor trailer overturned off a side road. Among its cargo which had survived years exposed to the elements were sealed containers of powdered drink mix packets. Fruit punch. Apple cider. Tea. And hot chocolate. One just had to add water and enjoy.

Enjoy...

It was odd to think that something so simple, and so common in the old world, could bring momentary happiness and satisfaction still. I figured that it was the normalcy of the act—drinking a favorite beverage. All it took to reconnect to a past pleasure was that. Perhaps we would begin producing something like it in the future. There was talk of restarting different industries on scales we could manage. Automobile production using refurbished parts from the countless wrecks strewn about the landscape. A town-wide cellular phone system. Even an air service, if parts could be located to repair the three planes and two helicopters which had been grounded at the town's airport since before I'd arrived with Neil, Grace, and Krista.

There was much we could do, and would do, but at this moment, in our house, we were going to have a couple mugs of hot chocolate.

"I'd love some," I said.

Elaine kissed me, and then our daughter, before slipping into the kitchen and setting a kettle of water to boil. As I waited for her to return with the steaming mugs, I sat again, this time in the rocker Schiavo had vacated, Hope in my arms, asleep. I sensed every rise and fall of her breathing, every quickened beat of her heart as I held her against my chest. My daughter. The new love of my life.

"It's going to be all right," I said to her, my voice soft. "I promise."

It was a natural assurance to offer, even though my daughter could not process the words, or the meaning in them. But I meant what I said. If it was in my power to do so, no matter the cost or any obstacles facing me, I would leave this world for her better than it was at the moment she'd come into it. That was my purpose. I would die for her.

I would also kill for her.

Part Two

Signs

Fourteen

"What do you think you're doing?"

I asked the question, issued the challenge, almost too loud, risking that I would wake our baby in the room just across the hall. But as I returned to our bedroom after a quick shower, what I found deserved no less a reaction than what I offered.

"Getting strong," Elaine answered on the upstroke of a pushup, elbows tucked close to her ribcage.

"For what? A triathlon?"

She pumped her body up a half dozen more times as I watched, incredulous.

"You just had a baby."

"I had a baby two weeks ago."

"I remember," I said. "I was there."

She angled her head toward me, flashing a look, *that* kind of look, one that both scolded and reassured at the same time. I'd grown accustomed to the visual cues Elaine wielded like arrows from a quiver. This was her '*I love you but back off*' look. The smart thing to do now would be to back off and let her finish her workout.

I wasn't that smart.

"All I'm suggesting is that you don't have to be super woman."

The sun hadn't yet risen and already she was up after a night of what could be generously termed sleep interrupted by feedings, and she was pushing herself to achieve the level of physical fitness she'd maintained before getting pregnant. I had no doubt that she could, and that she would, but her drive to do so while also caring for a newborn was concerning.

That she was ignoring that very concern was, also, pissing me off more than just a little.

"Elaine..."

"I put extra gloves in your pack," my wife informed me as she transitioned from pushups to sit-ups, hopping to a crouch and swinging her legs between her arms until she was flat on her back. "And a scarf."

I flashed a look that she missed, because if she'd glimpsed it her workout might have changed to her landing a roundhouse kick across my jaw.

"I just don't want you to do too much while I'm gone," I said.

"You're going to be away for, what, twelve hours? I can manage half a day."

Putting it that way, my worry did sound more than a bit ludicrous.

"Okay," I said. "I get it. I get it. Just..."

She didn't pause her rapid fire execution of crunches as she looked to me, waiting for what gem I might speak to begin digging myself still deeper into the hole I was already neck deep in.

"No bench pressing the pickup," I said.

With a stone cold expression as her face bobbed up and down with her quickly folding torso she gave me her answer.

"I can't make any promises."

How could I not love that?

* * *

The Humvee idled in the street as I stood on the porch with the first love of my life.

"Give Hope a kiss for me when she wakes up," I said.

In advance of that, Elaine kissed me, for a long moment. I half expected Schiavo to order Hart to lean on the vehicle's horn to break up our dawn make out session.

"Be careful," Elaine said as she eased back from our embrace.

It was a natural admonition to offer, and she'd said the same to me on many occasions, and me to her, but it never failed to remind me that it marked a point of separation. She would not be there to watch my back, nor I hers. It was an unusual but necessary fact of life that occurred from time to time.

"I'll be back tonight," I assured her.

"I know."

There was no horn blaring behind, but a quick surge in the Humvee's engine signaled that Hart was revving it to get my attention without waking the neighborhood.

"Gotta go," I said.

She gave me a last, soft kiss on the cheek and I lifted my backpack, carrying it and my AR down the walkway to the waiting military vehicle. I slid my gear into the back seat next to me and closed the door, watching out the window as we pulled away, Elaine waving in the glow of the porch light.

"Good morning, Fletch," Schiavo said from the front passenger seat, reaching back, a silvery thermos in hand. "Coffee?"

I shook off the offer, my last glimpse of Elaine, of our house, ending as Hart steered us around the corner. Schiavo put the container of coffee in a holder that had been added to the Spartan dash, a stack of disposable cups next to it.

"Actually, fill me up," I said.

She poured me a generous cup and handed it back. I sipped the steaming black liquid in silence as we headed for the highway.

"We'll have you back for a late supper," Schiavo told me, very obviously sensing the reason for my mildly sullen mood.

"Fletch..."

"Yes, Trey?"

Hart glanced back from his place at the wheel, just quick enough that I caught his very true and boyish smile. That one so young was charged with keeping men and women alive in combat still amazed me, but I'd seen him do just that. Schiavo was here because of his quick and steady treatment after being wounded as we sailed toward Juneau. Here, though, he was offering something else that could soothe pain—words.

"I didn't get a chance to congratulate you," Hart said.

"Thanks."

"It's great to have something like Hope to come home to, eh?"

The medic's words brought a smile to my face. What was that cliché? Absence made the heart grow fonder?

Damn straight, it did.

"You got that right," I said.

We left town and drove east as the sun rose on this new day we'd been granted.

Fifteen

Remote sat along Highway 42, two lanes of blacktop that wound inland from coastal Oregon. The town's most notable feature was an old covered bridge that crossed Sandy Creek, a minor stream that spilled into the Coquille River just south of the highway. The span had long ago ceased to function as a thoroughfare and was, at some point, converted into a pedestrian crossing and attraction of sorts, with historical markers and picnic benches beneath its peaked roof.

Schiavo and I strolled carefully onto it from the east side as Hart stood on the bank of the creek and tossed stones into the babbling water flowing past.

"It feels sturdy," the captain said.

It did. But my concern was the structure above. Weather had penetrated the shingled roof, the assault of wind and rain and snow unchecked and unrepaired for years now.

"Those timber supports will need to be rebuilt," I pointed out.

She looked at the growing damage over our heads and shook hers.

"This isn't a vital structure," she said. "Except for the wood that's left."

We'd be using that elsewhere in town, I suspected, to make repairs where they were needed most.

"Hart," Schiavo called out, and the specialist jogged up from the bank of the creek as we left the bridge and returned to the Humvee.

The medic drove us through the tiny hamlet, to scattered houses where we stopped and performed cursory inspections. Half of the buildings would require substantial work to make them safe for habitation. Most of the rest were usable with only repairs necessary to seal the houses against the weather. A few were beyond hope, and would need to be scavenged for materials to allow the remaining structures to survive.

"There's a cluster of buildings to the south," Schiavo said, pointing as we came down Sandy Creek Road.

A short drive from the bridge, across the highway and along Remote Lane, we reached a small white structure with a rusting old gas pump in front. A sign, faded by sun and the elements, was barely readable where it was mounted at the edge of a rickety overhang.

"Remote Store," Hart said, reading the signage as he pulled the Humvee to a stop in the road in front of the structure.

Another board dangled from a single nail, some letters painted upon it once identifying the building as a U.S. Post Office. Schiavo walked toward the building and pulled the board down. It fell to the soggy ground and snapped into three pieces.

"This is in rough shape," I said, surveying the outside. "New clapboards on at least the west facing wall. Same for the roof. We're going to need to find a fair amount of shingles to make this and the other buildings weather tight."

Schiavo nodded, but said nothing. Instead she stepped back, further into the narrow road, and gave the old store a once over from this new vantage point.

"What is it?" I asked.

"This would make a decent administrative center," she said. "Town Hall, garrison outpost, take your pick."

She wasn't wrong. If the building could be made safe and functional, its location, just far enough from the small residential cluster, would make it almost perfect for a group wary of the trappings of government. But for that to even be an issue, there would need to be that presence.

"Are you thinking of dividing the garrison?"

"I am," she told me.

Specialist Trey Hart perked up at that statement. He came around the front of the Humvee to face his leader.

"You're going to split us up, ma'am?"

"I think we should have someone here while people get settled," Schiavo told him. "Two of you."

Hart looked to the old store, seeming to contemplate the structure for a moment before facing the captain again.

"I'd like to volunteer," the young soldier announced.

Schiavo regarded him without voicing a thought one way or the other.

"It makes sense to have some medical personnel here," Hart told her. "A forty mile drive on that road is one hell of a haul for Commander Genesee to make a house call. And Mayor Allen..."

Doc Allen, to everyone who'd known him before he'd taken on the role of the town's elected leader, was well along in years. In the old world he would have been retired and enjoying leisurely walks and breakfasts on the porch with his wife. His late wife. Her absence had only seemed to bring the detriments of aging into more focus where it concerned him. He possessed all his mental faculties, but something in his spirit had most definitely been weakened. His shoulders stooped a bit more. His gaze was lucid but lackluster. In a pinch he could, and had, helped Commander Genesee in the hospital. How much longer that would hold true was not certain.

"He's got a point," I said.

Highway 42 was passable. We'd had to cut and push a few fallen trees from the roadway to clear the way forward, but the pavement was sketchy at best along several stretches. Until we could manage to make repairs, which could take months, the battered road was going to be the only reasonable lifeline between Bandon and the new settlement.

"Okay," Schiavo said, granting his request.

Another member of the garrison would certainly volunteer to join Hart in this temporary assignment, leaving the captain free from having to choose.

"Should we check out your new billet, specialist?" Schiavo asked.

Hart smiled and led the way into the old store.

There wasn't much to see inside. Anything not part of the actual building had been scavenged. Bits of trash and glass were scattered about, remnants of some previous investigation of the premises.

"Your thoughts, Fletch?"

I'd already begun thumping the walls by the time Schiavo solicited my opinion, as she had on the other houses and outbuildings we'd scouted already.

"I'm not seeing anything too bad," I told her. "Except for the exterior items, this is in surprisingly good shape. Better than just about any we've looked at."

There was even some glass still in the windows. I looked through the one on the eastern wall, a long, narrow structure just outside across a swath of muddy ground, maybe fifty feet from the garrison's new outpost. I'd noticed it on the way in, a garage or workshop of some sort, I thought, the wide wooden door that faced the street splintered and peeled back to reveal a dark interior.

"I'm going to go check that building next door," I told Schiavo and Hart. "We might be able to borrow from it to refurbish this exterior."

Schiavo gave me a nod and I left them, crossing the space to the front of what I was certain now had been some sort of storage building. Instinctively I readied my grip on my AR as I stepped into the opening where the main door had once hung. There was no expectation of a threat from within. Or from anywhere, for that matter. Whatever intrusion there'd been back in Bandon, this location, forty miles away, was too distant to serve as any haven for those who'd perpetrated the break-ins.

For an instant, though, I flashed back to my encounter with the starving grizzly north of my refuge in Montana. That creature had come through a sturdy wall as I searched for a usable automotive battery, and only a few fortunate shots from the very weapon I still carried saved me that day.

There would be no bear here. I knew that. But the ingrained need to be ready took over as I kept my finger alongside and just above the trigger and retrieved a small flashlight from my pocket, its narrow beam cutting across the trashed space, revealing what had once been an old pickup, just frame and rusted cab now resting on the gravel floor. Old oil drums lay on their side near the west wall, a door there closed, windows nearby broken out. I scanned the rafters above, all seeming solid, as did the exposed interior wall framing.

The remainder of the space was just a picked over conglomeration of open crates, broken containers, and shelving tipped and piled in one corner. Nothing of much use or interest lay anywhere within the four walls. I thought that until I my flashlight beam swept a spot on the floor just behind a pair of upright 55 gallon drums.

I froze, the light fixed on the cleared-out spot, no trash or discarded items littering the floor there, the area purposely swept clean. But not empty.

Two rocks...

That was what had seized my attention. Two small rocks. They were arranged close to each other, with a narrow space left between them. I stepped close and crouched, shifting my light to illuminate the sides of the rocks that faced each other. Each was scarred black. Charred. By some small but intense fire that had burned between them. Like a flame from some chemical fuel tablet.

Exactly how Olin had heated his food at his hideaway near Bandon. Two rocks, a fuel source, in a place that provided shelter, and cover.

He'd been here. The man who'd murdered my friend had crouched right where I was and tended to his covert fire. But when? Before he came to Bandon, or after he'd done his damage and slipped away?

"Fletch..."

It was Schiavo. She'd come through the open front of the building and was sweeping her flashlight across the space. I stood so the beam could find me.

"What is it?" she asked. "What did you find?"

I motioned her over and showed her the compact cooking arrangement. She puzzled at my interest in it, but only until I spoke.

"Olin cooked just like this where he holed up," I said. "Exactly like this."

She stepped a bit past me and crouched to examine the rocks, dragging a finger gently across one's top.

"There's a layer of dust," she said, scanning the otherwise unremarkable space and its hodgepodge of discarded contents. "This could have been here for months, Fletch."

I knew that. But it was a sign, a concrete indication, that Tyler Olin hade come through this very place.

"He's not here," Schiavo said, standing again. "There's no reason for him to be here."

"Of course there is. BA Four Twelve."

The biological agent that was cousin to BA 411, the engineered cause of the blight. A companion disease that would do to humans what eleven had done to plant life the world over.

"We don't have it," Schiavo reminded me.

"No," I said. "But he doesn't know that."

Neil's brief message hidden in Krista's drawings had confirmed Four Twelve's existence, and gave simple directions on how to mimic it, an act which had allowed me to threaten the Unified Government's forces into ending their siege of Bandon and fleeing. The same message had also promised that the real sample of the deadly bioweapon was somewhere safe. But Neil had been killed before he could share the location, if he'd been inclined to do so at all.

"He could still be looking for it," I told the captain.

She eyed me for a moment, then nodded as her gaze dipped briefly.

"He told you, didn't he?"

"Who?" I asked.

"Martin," she answered. "He told you he thinks you were specifically targeted."

I hadn't considered that the man had told his wife about what he'd discovered while investigating any link between the break-ins. But it did not surprise me that he had.

"He thinks the other burglaries were diversions," I said.

"Fletch..."

"Olin wants Four Twelve," I said. "He asked where it was when he called my house."

"And then he disappeared," Schiavo reminded me. "What is that, nine months ago? Nine and a half? If he'd wanted to keep looking for it, he wouldn't have taken almost a year off."

Tyler Olin was a patient man. He'd crossed the desolate country to seek out our shared friend. I expect he'd thought

Neil would hand over the sample of Four Twelve he'd spirited away from the government, but something had convinced him that his old partner in spying was not going to be so cooperative. So he killed him.

He killed my friend.

"Fletch, if he was here, he's long gone. There's zero evidence of any other conclusion."

"And Martin?"

She considered her words for a moment, choosing carefully.

"Martin cares. About you. About the town. About everyone. That makes him..."

"Wrong?"

Schiavo hadn't considered that challenge to the opinion she was offering, and, in the end, she wouldn't counter it.

"Jittery," she said. "He sees shadows, and things in the shadows."

"He wasn't wrong about Quincy," I reminded Schiavo, her husband's singular role in unmasking the Unified Government's traitor in our midst undeniable.

"I know," Schiavo said. "I know. But this isn't that. Okay? This is a couple of rocks and my husband showing concern for a friend. Don't let the two combine to create some reality that simply doesn't exist."

There was enough doubt in what I was thinking, and what Martin had suggested, to put any true fear aside. Add to that the certainty with which Schiavo was trying to soothe any fears on my part, and I had to admit the unlikelihood of what I was thinking. Tyler Olin wasn't here now. He wasn't anywhere to be seen now. There were no other signs that he was, or had been.

"Okay," I said, sweeping my boot across the dusty floor to knock the pair of rocks away. "Let's—"

"Captain!"

It was Hart. He stood at the doorway, peering in, his gaze then shifting to something off to his right.

"You need to see this."

We moved quickly to the door and joined Hart outside, each of us looking to the east at a column of dense black smoke rising in the distance.

"Camas Valley?" Schiavo wondered aloud.

The direction was right, maybe just a bit north of due east. Even the distance seemed possible. But it would have to be one hell of a fire for the smoke column to loft as high as it was.

"That's ten miles," Hart said. "Something big is burning."

"Thank God everything is wet," I said.

The blizzard had left coastal Oregon and points inland blanketed in white. The two weeks since had left a soggy mess where the unusual abundance of snow had melted, only a few patches of it remaining in deeply shaded spots. Were this two months later, with the dead forest dried out, any substantial fire, combined with even a slight wind, could sweep across the landscape, endangering every town that remained standing. Including Remote.

"We need to check it out," Schiavo said.

I looked to the sun, arcing past noon to the west already. We had the time to do a quick run toward Camas Valley, maybe fifteen miles by the highway, before darkness would make a return trip to Bandon treacherous on the spotty road.

"Specialist, let them know what we're doing."

Hart heeded his captain's order and hustled to the Humvee, operating the radio from the front seat for a moment before returning.

"Ma'am, I'm not sure they can hear."

"Too much terrain in the way," I said.

The rise and fall of the landscape, made up of hills large and small, was, at least in our present position, preventing any direct radio communication.

"They may not be acknowledging," Schiavo said. "But they may be hearing us. We'll transmit along the way while we check it out."

"You sure about this?"

My challenge, mild as it was, was acceptable. I wasn't one of Captain Angela Schiavo's troops. But that didn't stop Hart from shooting me a quick look that doubted the wisdom of my choice to do so.

"Do we really need to know what's burning?" she asked, voicing the crux of my doubt. "No."

"But you want to," I said.

"That's out of the ordinary," she said, pointing at the twisting ribbon of smoke rising ever higher. "I like ordinary. Ordinary things don't surprise. Right now I'm surprised that something in this soggy landscape found a way to ignite. Aren't you?"

I was. And she was right—ordinary, as boring as it might be, was good. It was safe. This was something else.

"How long to Camas Valley?" Schiavo asked.

"Thirty minutes," Hart Said. "Probably closer to forty five considering the condition of the highway."

"Not with me at the wheel," Schiavo said, and started off toward the driver's side of the Humvee.

"Shotgun," I said.

"Be my guest," Hart said.

We joined the captain in the vehicle and she pulled away from what would become the garrison outpost in Remote. Back on the highway she kept a lead foot on the accelerator, steering us along the winding road toward the smoke billowing skyward beyond the hills.

Sixteen

We estimated we were within a mile of the origin of the smoke when we could go no further.

"Wonderful," Schiavo said as she slowed the Humvee and stopped it a dozen yards short of the obstruction, thumping the steering wheel lightly in frustration. "Just wonderful."

"I'll check it out," I said.

I left the passenger door of the idling vehicle open as I approached the stout, fallen tree that lay across the two lanes of blacktop. It had split into sections upon impact, the blight long ago robbing it of any interior structural integrity. But those pieces, seven to ten feet in length, and each a full thirty inches in diameter, were multi-ton hunks of dead wood that would be difficult to push clear using the Humvee, even if attempting such was wise.

Which it wasn't. We still hadn't been able to definitively reach Bandon via the radio since setting out from Remote, and all we needed was to disable our means of transportation trying to bash our way through the remnants of the massive fir in our path. An up close look at the monster tree only confirmed that it wasn't going anywhere, which meant the cause of the smoke ahead near Camas Valley would have to remain a mystery. If it were as small as the few pines we'd had to clear on our way to Remote we might have been able—

I didn't actually see what caused my thoughts to stutter. I sensed it. And heard it. Something that penetrated the total silence which had become so normal in the new world. Aside from a slight breeze, barely registering as a whisper, there was nothing.

Except for the sound. It was indefinable. Ambiguous. But that it had reached my ears at all was the fact that gave it importance. There should be nothing in the woods to make such a hushed disturbance, but there was.

I turned away from the fallen tree, shaking my head to feign interested disgust with our dilemma. At the same time, as I walked back toward the Humvee, I took hold of my AR's grip, eyes scanning the dead woods to either side of the highway. Climbing back in next to Schiavo, I pulled the door shut and switched the selector of my rifle from safe to burst.

"We've got company," I said.

Behind, I heard Hart shift positions in the back seat, bringing his own weapon up.

"Where?" Schiavo asked.

"I don't know."

"One person?"

I shook my head at her probing. And for the first time I noticed something odd about the fallen tree. Many a blighted pine, or fir, or aspen, or any number of trees had toppled over the years, giving in to the rot and wind and shifting soils. We'd encountered several of those after leaving Bandon. This particular tree, though, had been the tallest of a stand just to the left side of the road. Any of the others near it which might have fallen would not have completely blocked the way forward.

"Someone took that tree down," I said.

"We're getting out of here," Schiavo said. "Fletch, get on the radio and report our situation and location."

I reached for the radio, but never had the chance to follow her directive.

Seventeen

My hand was on the mic to put out a warning broadcast when the explosion shook the vehicle, jolting it from the right rear. It was not a direct impact, and there'd been no sound of an incoming rocket or missile. I'd experienced that close up, while defending the northern perimeter from the Unified Government forces. There, an incoming LAW or RPG had taken out the bunker we'd been holding, almost killing Enderson in the process. This sound, and the resultant effect, was not that.

But it was part of an attack.

"Ambush!"

Hart shouted from the rear seat, looking back just as I did, both of us seeing a pair of tall, dead fir trees collapsing across a spot on the road we'd just passed, blocking any route of retreat. Large clouds of dust and dirt billowed at the base of the trees, kicked up by the detonations which had felled them.

"We've gotta get out of here," Schiavo said.

She swung the Humvee hard left, searching for a way around the single tree that blocked our way forward. The left side of the bulky vehicle rolled off the asphalt and onto the soft shoulder before Schiavo stopped and shook her head at the wall of dead woods ahead, the spaces between trees too narrow to navigate.

"Out!"

She gave the command as she threw herself out the left side of the vehicle. I was ready to do the same on my side, but a volley of rounds peppering the lightly armored exterior sent me left, over the driver's seat. I found myself on the damp earth, Schiavo to my left and Hart, who'd just bailed from the back seat, to my right.

"Where are they?" Hart asked, his weapon ready.

Schiavo didn't wait to offer any answer, or any guess. She rose quickly up from the cover of the Humvee and squeezed off three bursts from her M4, spreading her fire along the line of grey pines that stepped down toward the Coquille River beyond the road.

"This is not a great position," I said, not shouting yet.

In fact, it was an awful position, for either defense or offense. Behind us the woods stepped up the gentle slope of a hill. Any retreat that way would be a treacherous dash up soggy earth where fire from across the highway could chew us to pieces.

Bam!

One of the Humvee's tires blew from incoming rounds, then another, the heavy vehicle settling toward its passenger side.

"There goes our ride," Hart said.

He and I both popped up almost simultaneously, firing across the highway as Schiavo reloaded her weapon.

"Reminds me of Mary Island," I said as Hart and I dropped back down to cover. "Before you all showed up."

Rogue Russian forces had laid siege to the lighthouse on that dollop of land off the southern coast of Alaska. We'd been surrounded, outnumbered, facing almost certain annihilation, until Schiavo's unit had arrived by helicopter, decimating the invaders and saving Elaine, Neil, and me.

Here, though, there would be no cavalry miraculously appearing out of thin air.

"We have to move," Schiavo said. "Textbook says attack into the ambush."

"I'm not too fond of that book right now, ma'am."

Hart wasn't disagreeing with his captain. He was simply addressing the reality which often countered standard tactics. This situation was one of those instances. A headlong rush across the road into fire, even if our present position was untenable, made no more sense. We'd simply be dead sooner.

As it turned out, our situation changed. And not for the better.

"You hear that?" Hart asked.

We all did. The absence of sound was just as jarring as the staccato impacts of rounds chewing into the Humvee. The fire from across the road stopped, all at once, multiple points of origin going quiet simultaneously. That was an ominous sign.

"They're coordinated," Schiavo said, voicing the disquieting realization I'd just come to.

Hart shifted further toward the back of the Humvee, covering as much of the western flank as he could. But it was not from that direction that the final assault came.

"Behind!"

Schiavo shouted the warning and brought her M4 up, spinning away from the Humvee to take aim at figures charging in our direction through the ranks of dead trees. She fired a pair of bursts and backed toward Hart, not a lick of cover anywhere for us.

"Shift west!"

The captain's order was clear, but impossible to follow in the second after she'd given it. A volley of fire from the sloping woods tore into the side of the Humvee, spraying me with bits of ricocheted lead, hot metal searing one side of my face. I dropped to the ground and began firing from a prone position, taking aim at everything moving between the trees.

"Movement across the road!" Hart reported, opening up with his weapon at the rear of the vehicle. "They've got us surrounded!"

We had to move, and we couldn't move. The only cover we had was bad cover, and it was right where we'd planted ourselves. I was firing north, along with Schiavo, up the hill where a banzai charge could materialize at any moment. Hart was trying to cover west and south, with the rear of the Humvee both cover and an obstacle to his ability to do so. One quick move from the east and we would be overrun.

PTHUP!

The sound was almost hollow, but it came from somewhere close, above us and to the east, from the very crest of the hill that overlooked the site of the battle.

"Grenade!"

Schiavo shouted the warning and hit the dirt, keeping her weapon in play and directed at our attackers. Hart made himself as small a target as possible. I was already flat on the ground, but scanning the area I could see no evidence of a grenade being thrown at us.

Then I realized, in a flash of memory, that nothing had been thrown—it had been fired. An explosive round, from a launcher slung beneath an enemy rifle, or fired from a dedicated weapon, such as the venerable M-79, was sailing our way. Schiavo had recognized the sound of the projectile being fired.

The sound of it impacting both startled and heartened us all.

BOOM!

The explosion ripped through the trees on the slope above, screams accompanying the blast. A pair of injured individuals, both men, stumbled toward us, bleeding but still wielding their weapons, an AK-47 and a bolt action rifle. Hart and I fired, bursts from each of our weapons striking the man with the AK. He dropped to the ground and rolled down the slope until a tree stopped his motion. The man with the bolt action, looking like a plain-Jane hunting rifle topped with a cheap scope, tried to bring his rifle to bear with a grotesquely injured right arm, but a follow up burst from the garrison's young medic sent him reeling, head flopping backward, what had been his face and head no longer resembling anything human.

"Who's shooting at them?" Hart asked.

Schiavo crawled fast behind me toward the front of the Humvee and took aim with her M4 under the leaning nose of the vehicle.

"Across the road is taking fire," she said.

Someone on the crest of the hill, and from other vantage points was laying into whoever had ambushed us. I'd been wrong—somehow, inexplicably, the cavalry had arrived.

"North again!"

It was Hart shouting. Both Schiavo and I redirected to the sloping woods where we'd just dropped two enemy. Three more were racing down the hill toward us, a mix of weapons firing wildly—pistols, shotguns, another AK. We returned fire, but before our volleys could have any effect another grenade detonated, almost dead center along their ragged line, shredding the middle enemy, a woman, from the waist down. Her fellow fighters, both men, each took full sprays of shrapnel, crumbling to the ground and sliding to a stop just beyond the nearest trees.

More streams of automatic fire poured down from the crest of the hill, sweeping the slope until there were no more sounds of battle. Behind us, on the far side of the Humvee, whoever had been firing at us from the forest across the highway was now silenced. We lay still, covering every direction we could as a few single shots rang out from above. Aimed fire that had a name which Schiavo uttered.

"Kill shots."

Someone above was dispatching any fighters who were wounded and still moving.

"Don't move!"

The voice was male, shouted from the crest, but nowhere we could directly see.

"We're coming down to you!"

We...

"Captain, what do we do?"

Hart was asking one of the most basic questions a commander could answer—fight or give up. The difference here, though, was it didn't seem to me that the actions we'd just witnessed, being saved by unknown forces who could just as easily have killed us, made either option prudent.

"We wait, Specialist," Schiavo said, giving the order I would have were I in her shoes.

A half a minute passed before we heard movement. From behind us, on the far side of the Humvee first. Then from the slope that ran down from the crest of the hill. Schiavo stood slowly, her weapon ready, but held low.

"Stand up, gentlemen," she said.

Hart and I did just that, mimicking her ready, but relaxed posture. As soon as I was upright I glanced behind and saw a line of people, two women and four men, standing near the guardrail just beyond the far edge of the highway. They, too, took an almost casual stance, rifles and one Squad Automatic Weapon slung, no fear about them.

"Fletch..."

Schiavo's voice drew my attention back to the slope we faced. Another half dozen fighters emerged there from the trees, well-armed, not a matching uniform among the ragtag group. But they looked healthy, not thin, which didn't surprise me. Any who'd lasted this long through the blight had surpassed the time of hunger and starvation. They'd found a way to survive, though not thrive. Their faces, their eyes, told me that. I saw no joy, no relief, even though there should have been some hint of such after a successful engagement. But all there was were stares, fixed on us. Maybe some distrust in them. Or disinterest. I couldn't tell which, but I suspected we'd be made aware of just what they thought of us in short order.

"I'm Lo," one of the men who'd just come down the slope said as his group approached and stopped facing us. "We're not going to hurt you."

"Who was that who attacked us?" Schiavo asked the man.

He seemed to consider her question for a moment, then wiped a smear of dirt from his brow and pointed toward the east.

"We've got to get you to town," Lo told us. "It's a couple mile walk so we should get started."

Behind, I heard movement. Taking a quick glance I saw the element of fighters across the road form up in a loose line aimed east, waiting for orders to move, it appeared.

"You all ready?"

Lo's question was more of a suggestion. There were no weapons pointed in our direction to prod us along, but the request didn't seem all that optional, either. Schiavo, too, knew that, and she looked to Hart, and then to me before nodding toward the road.

"Let's get going," she said.

Hart led off, Schiavo right behind. I brought up our rear, with the entire group who'd come down the hill falling in behind me. We moved onto the road and followed the other part of the unit who'd saved us, heading east and a bit north.

"Are we going to Camas Valley?" I asked Lo, who was directly behind me.

He didn't offer a reply, choosing instead to keep the pace up, staring past me, his AK held low and ready. One fight might have been won, but I sensed that the man trailing me, and those with him, were ready for another if it came to them.

Why didn't they disarm us?

That question rattled about my thoughts as we moved up the highway. It was a fair assumption to make that they had no intention of killing us, or holding us prisoner. Add to that the fact that they'd risked themselves to save us, and the situation was as confusing as it was strange.

"Listen, Lo, just who—"

"Fletch," Schiavo said, cutting me off as she glanced back. "Let's just get to where they're taking us."

I couldn't tell if she was attempting to avoid any escalation of the situation by shutting down my very logical question, or if she had picked up on something that had settled any worry for her. It didn't matter, though. She was right to interrupt and quash what could have turned into a badgering demand for an explanation. We were outnumbered, and those who held that sway over us seemed to really want us to go with them.

So we walked, leaving Bandon even further behind than it already was.

Eighteen

Not quite a mile down the road, with Camas Valley just out of view, we came upon an overturned truck, lying just off the highway in a gully that ran alongside, the inferno which had engulfed it dying down.

"Who set the fire?" I asked, momentarily breaking the directive Schiavo had gently given.

"Not us," Lo answered.

It wasn't a crash, I could tell. The old stake bed, which had probably once hauled apples or pears from some nearby orchard, was missing its driveshaft and one rear wheel, neither of which lay anywhere nearby. The faint stench of old diesel, almost sour in its bite, hung in the air as we moved past on the far side of the road. Someone had doused the vehicle with the useless fuel and set it ablaze. And I had an idea why.

"Was that meant for us?" I asked.

Schiavo shot me a warning look, but Lo answered without taking any umbrage at what I was asking.

"It worked, didn't it?"

It wasn't meant as a slap at the captain, but the way she turned away made it plain to me that she'd taken it that way. Her insistence had led us to seek out the origin of the smoke, and that had brought us directly into the ambush. But that was the risk every leader took when leading. What was worse, though, was making *no* decision. Schiavo had never suffered from that deficiency, and I was glad for that.

We left the burning wreck behind. A half hour later we entered Camas Valley, a deserted hamlet we'd patrolled on a few occasions before. Except, it was most certainly not deserted now. From a pair of houses just off the highway, one on each side, sentries stepped out into view. As we continued on those fighters joined us.

"They've reoccupied the town," Hart said.

"No," Lo said, hearing his statement. "We've been here from the start."

I looked back to the man making the claim, his tired eyes meeting mine as he allowed only the smallest smile to curl his lips.

"You just didn't see us," he said.

If that was true, if would have meant a highly coordinated effort to stay concealed from the scavengers who'd certainly come through town, not to mention those of us from Bandon.

We angled off the main road and followed a narrow street to what was still identified as the town's school, heading for a door that a tall woman was holding open, semi-auto Remington shotgun slung across her chest. The lead element of our column split off, as did those behind Lo.

"There's a room just inside to stow your weapons and gear," he said. "Gina will show you where."

Schiavo stopped us just outside the door and looked to the man who'd led us here. Gina laid a hand loosely atop her shotty's pistol grip, more than a hint of impatience about her.

"I'm not exactly comfortable giving up our weapons," she said.

"The people in there aren't real comfortable with you having them," Lo countered.

For a very brief moment, hardly more than a few seconds, Schiavo weighed the choice facing her, which wasn't really any choice at all. Still, she had to voice her displeasure at the requirement. Doing anything less would project weakness, and I was pretty certain that lack of virtue would not serve us well in what, or who, we were about to encounter.

"I assume they'll be unarmed as well," Schiavo said.

"That's correct," Lo confirmed.

To that she nodded. Lo turned away, leaving us with the armed woman at the door.

"Logan is good people," Gina said.

Logan. Long for Lo. Not Lothario, or some similarly odd moniker. I had to concur with what the woman had shared—he did seem decent, at least on the face of what he had allowed us to see.

"And everyone else?" Hart asked.

Gina didn't answer right away, shrugging after a moment's consideration.

"Most," she said, tipping her head toward the open door.

Most...

This was the real world, after all. Not some gathering of saints. Our town had its share of residents with less than stellar moral fiber. But not many. I could count those on a single hand and still have a couple fingers left over.

Hart went through first, Schiavo and I right behind. Gina followed us and pointed to a long table. We laid our weapons out there and shed the scant amount of gear we'd had on us when bailing from the Humvee.

"Right through there," Gina said, pointing to a doorway with no door.

Even in the scant light of a single bulb glowing above I could see that stairs descended toward some brighter location. Before we moved I let my gaze play over the space we stood in, reconciling it with what I'd seen of the structure outside, which appeared to be a modest sized gymnasium, or a multi-purpose room. Some serious modification had clearly taken place to what should have been a very open interior. It had been segmented, at least the part I was able to see.

"They're waiting," Gina said.

Schiavo moved first. Hart followed her through the opening and down the stairs. I hesitated just a bit, fairly certain that no school in this area had been constructed with a basement beneath their gym. Such a space could be a place to hide. Or to hide things that were done to others.

Nineteen

They hadn't seen the blight coming. No, their planning was for the end of the world in a more general sense. Economic collapse. Nuclear war. A North Korean EMP burst. The cause of civilization's unraveling wasn't important—their preparation for the result was.

"How many of you are there?"

Schiavo posed the question to the lean, tall man seated across from us. He was not armed, nor were the two others who stood to his right, one man and one woman. Then again, neither were we, giving this meeting without arms the feeling of some tense, benign summit. He'd started off by sharing that vague description of the how and why they'd managed to survive, hardly enough to explain the success they'd had at not being discovered by our patrols.

"You want information on our numbers," the tall man said, suspicion plain in his restatement of the captain's inquiry. "You want to know our strength. Is that it?"

There was bait in the man's challenge. But there was also justifiable wariness. Before him were three strangers, two of them wearing the uniform of the country many believed had abandoned them. Or worse.

"This isn't some reconnaissance," Schiavo assured him. "Mr...?"

She was trying to shift the tone of the exchange. Bring it back from the verge of some accusatory confrontation.

"I'm Captain Angela Schiavo," she said, gesturing to me and Hart next. "This is Eric Flet—"

"Eric Fletcher and Specialist Trey Hart," the man said. "We know who you are," the woman standing next to him told us. "We know all about you."

The expression of knowledge halted the conversation for a moment, the admission of the seemingly impossible more than a little unsettling. I flashed back to the detailed, annotated map found with the radio in my house after my confrontation with the intruders.

"My name is Dalton," the tall man said, breaking the raging silence. "This is Moira and Ansel."

Singular names, and nothing more, to add to Lo and Gina. But it was something he was offering. A tiny window into their world. Their isolated, darkened world.

"We have just over eight hundred residents in Bandon," I said, and Dalton's knowing gaze shifted to me. "But you know that, too, don't you?"

"We've been watching you," Moira said, some restrained ferocity in her voice, her manner. "Since the collapse."

"You have the cure," Ansel said.

"It's not our cure," Schiavo told him. "You're welcome to it. We have seeds. Livestock."

Over the time since Bandon had begun its recovery, with deliveries of animals and plant stock from the *Rushmore*, a few things had gone missing. A half dozen chickens over three months. A goat. Two pigs. A fruit tree toppled and its bounty gone. All were things we'd assumed were just unfortunate events. Animals escaping their pens and coops. Wind uprooting apple trees. Not to mention the intrusions into private homes, including mine.

Now, though, we knew better. Or I did.

"I believe they already have what they need," I said. "Or want."

Schiavo thought for a moment on what I was suggesting, her gaze fixing hard on Dalton again as she made the same connection I had a moment earlier, a subtle disappointment about her. Our town had been penetrated, covertly, on numerous occasions. Likely more than even we realized.

"You stole from us," she said. "You didn't need to do that."

Dalton fixed hard on me, his look somewhere between harsh and angry. After a moment he simply shook his head.

"We don't need to steal," Dalton said.

"We're supplied for years," Moira told us.

A slight shift of Dalton's head, his gaze angling obliquely toward her, expressed some displeasure at the information she'd just offered. She quieted and straightened, coming to some self-imposed attention as her leader, their leader, looked to us again.

"The hiders have been stealing from you," Dalton said.

"The hiders?" Schiavo asked.

"You didn't think you were alone," Dalton said, allowing just a hint of a grin. "That's precious."

"Who are these hiders?"

Schiavo's repetition of her question, not quite to the level of a demand, turned Dalton's expression slack again just as the single lightbulb in the room flickered, drawing all gazes to it.

"Ansel..."

Dalton's simple speaking of the man's name sent him from the room. As he left he looked toward me, a covert obviousness in the way his gaze tracked to mine. I'd noticed the same hidden interest when I'd entered the room with the others, and again when he'd directed us to our chairs. This last look he gave me, though, I sensed something in it. I wondered if we'd met somewhere in the old world. There had been enough men about his age who'd crossed my path in the business I was in. Workers, subcontractors, clients, inspectors. He could have been any one of those. Or, just some nameless guy I'd had a random conversation with in line at the grocery store.

Or, he could be no one at all.

"We have power issues at times," Dalton said. "The whole world's become the third world."

"Not Bandon," I said.

"Not yet," Dalton countered.

After my brief exchange with the man who was either our savior or our captor, or both, Schiavo laid her arms on the table and leaned forward, toward him, annoyance now clear in her manner.

"If you wouldn't mind answering my question," Schiavo said. "Who the hell are the hiders?"

Dalton let her insistence simmer for just a few seconds, then nodded to Moira.

"Some are like us," Moira explained. "Survivors who laid low. Went underground. Just hung on and clawed and scratched to stay alive."

"But they're not our problem," Dalton said. "They're yours."

"And why is that?"

Dalton regarded Schiavo for a few seconds after she posed the question, as if he was mildly astonished that she even needed to ask it. Then, his air of judgment eased, and he nodded, confirming some conclusion he'd just come to.

"You've been in the bubble too long," Dalton said.

"Excuse me?" Schiavo pressed him.

The light dimmed further, then turned bright again with steady brilliance.

"Things have been good for you," Dalton said, allowing a slight modification of his statement. "Relatively. You have numbers. You have authority, perceived as it might be. You have food. Medical personnel. Vehicles. Fuel. Power."

He paused there, seeming to wait for Schiavo, Hart, or myself to signal that we understood the premise he was laying out. None of us did.

"I could go on, but there's no point," Dalton said, relaxing against the backrest of his chair. "You're too busy trying to recreate the world to realize you're drawing a target on your back."

"How are we doing that?" Schiavo asked.

Dalton smiled, shaking his head as he glanced briefly away.

"Any survivors, this is Bandon, we have food, shelter, and medical services," Moira said. "Come to us. We're waiting."

She'd parroted perfectly Krista's daily broadcasts.

"It's no different than when that boy was squawking on about Eagle One," Dalton said.

The dismissive way in which he spoke of Micah, of her husband's late child, brought a visible pique to Schiavo's expression. She seemed on the verge of challenging Dalton, of setting him straight about the boy, but I was the one who could not dam my response.

"That squawking boy is the reason we're alive," I said. "And the reason you'll be alive a few years from now if you have any sense."

His attention had been almost laser-focused on Schiavo, but now Dalton very obviously angled his gaze to me. Anything resembling a smile, or any hint of amusement or joy, was gone from his face, just a harshness left in its place. A stare as cold as any I'd ever experienced.

"Is that so?"

His challenge to me was brief. Simple. And, I suspected, attached to some consequence which would befall me, maybe all of us, if I was not able to justify the verbal slap I'd just lobbed his way.

"Your supplies aren't unlimited," I told him. "I don't care how many cans of tuna and beans you have cached, it will run out."

In the short time we'd been in his presence, Dalton's subdued authoritarianism told me most of what I needed to know about his, and their, one glaring weakness—isolation. That state of being was their choice, even their plan, and he was clinging to it as if it were a lifeline. It was, in actuality, an anchor, one that was slowly, but certainly, dragging them toward the fate the rest of civilization had suffered.

"I don't see any green fields around here," I said. "I don't smell livestock. Or hear chickens. And I'm not even going to mention that cut on Moira's shoulder."

The woman reached up with her hand and laid it over the small bandage that had been affixed over some apparently minor wound just visible where the collar of her coat had shifted. A wound whose angry infection had reddened the skin beyond the sterile covering which attempted to protect it.

"We have doctors," Hart said. "Two of them."

Dalton didn't respond. But he did react. The look about him changed. In some way, I thought that it softened. Perhaps it was the recognition by a leader, however slight, that they could not provide all that their followers needed. That some necessities were beyond his ability to secure.

"Specialist Hart here is a medic," Schiavo said. "If you get him his gear, he can take a look at her wound."

"I don't need any—"

A simple raised hand cut her off. There was no anger in Dalton's gesture. Nor in his gaze. Instead I sensed contemplation. And Curiosity. And, very plainly, a wondering.

"And what do you want in return?" he asked.

I'd expected Schiavo to reply quickly. To assure him that there was no quid pro quo. No agenda in the offer.

But she did not do any of those things. She sat quietly for a moment, mulling his question. I was at a loss as to what she was doing. Or thinking. She seemed to know that, at that very instant, she was in a position of power, and for a person in her position, a leader, such an opportunity was impossible to ignore.

"All I want is for you to listen," Schiavo told him.

"To what?" Dalton asked.

Schiavo drew a slow breath, her chin rising ever so slightly.

"A proposal."

Twenty

Dalton listened to her, as we all did. When Schiavo was done, there was silence. And surprise. From all who'd heard her propose a formal alliance between Dalton's Camas Valley colony and Bandon.

"You don't have the authority to do what you just did," Dalton said.

He wasn't wrong. But in that knowledge, Schiavo had her opening.

"You're right," she said. "Our civilian leadership would have to formally offer what I have. We're not a dictatorship. But my word will carry weight."

Dalton had to know what Schiavo was saying was true. They knew enough about our town, its leadership structure, the way we adhered to basic laws, to realize that any suggestion by the military leader assigned to protect Bandon would be considered without hesitation. And likely acted upon.

"So?" Schiavo pressed.

"Throwing in with you would be throwing in with the institution that abandoned everybody," Moira said.

Dalton did not cut her off this time, giving credence to her wariness.

"We're not the government," I said.

Quickly, though, Schiavo clarified the statement I'd made.

"We're not *that* government," she said. "The institution you hold responsible is gone."

Dalton snickered.

"I wasn't making a joke," Schiavo told him.

"Not intentionally, I'm sure," Dalton countered, leaning forward and regarding Schiavo with something between pity and disbelief. "Do you seriously think that that bureaucratic behemoth just faded away? To be replaced by those pretenders that laid siege to you? If you do, then that bubble you've created to live in is thicker than I thought."

I couldn't tell if Schiavo was accepting his premise that some semblance of the United States government, president, representatives, judges, still existed somewhere, in some recognizable form, or if she was simply done trying to engage with the man. Whichever it was, she chose not to belabor the point.

"If our leadership approves of this, what can I tell them about your position on the proposal?"

It was a direct and simple question that Schiavo posed to the leader of the Camas Valley survivors. But the manner in which Dalton seemed to weigh his response, and the long, silent moment in which he did, hinted very strongly that any choice he made would be final. No committee, no council, no vote of his people would be required to give it the full effect of law. Apparently, he was the law.

"An alliance," Dalton said, nodding. "We help secure the area around your settlement at Remote, and you provide us with seeds and livestock."

"Agreed," Schiavo said.

Once more, Dalton went silent as he considered what he was agreeing to, some doubt creeping into his manner.

"It's not fair," the man told us.

For an instant. Schiavo let the frustration of his response show, her chest heaving with a breath that attempted to calm.

"Dalton, what we're offering is—"

"No," he said. "What you're offering is fair. What we'd be giving in return is not."

The three of us from Bandon exchanged quick looks, not certain of what Dalton was suggesting.

"Balance is important," he said. "It's crucial in life. In all things. Keeping your new settlement secure is not difficult. You saw what my people did today. We saw the smoke that was baiting you, and we knew what the hiders were going to do once you took that bait. So we acted."

I was beginning to understand what his point was, and where he was coming from.

"You've caused us no harm," Dalton said. "The hiders have. To allow them a victory over you..."

"It would upset the balance," I said.

"In their favor," he confirmed. "And that is not right. Just as this arrangement between us would be if we take more than we give."

Schiavo realized what he was saying now. We all did. More importantly, we were coming to see that there was something about Dalton we hadn't expected when first facing him just moments earlier—he was a man of honor. A deep honor, closely held, but foundational to his existence as a man. As a person.

"We have something I believe you you'll want," Dalton said.

It only took him a few minutes to tell us what that was, and how it was possible. When he'd finished, he stood, as did Schiavo, each reaching across the table to shake the other's hand.

"We'll have your vehicle repaired," Dalton said, glancing to his left. "Moira..."

She left to see that his promise was carried out.

"You'll be able to leave by morning," he told us.

"Our people will be worried," Schiavo said. "They'll definitely send a patrol out to look for us when we aren't back by nightfall."

Dalton nodded, understanding.

"Your radios can't reach from Remote," he said.

"And definitely not from here," I said.

"We have a transmitter and repeater you can use. It's tied into an antenna we concealed on a hill just west of here. That's how we've monitored your radios."

From beginning to now, the tone of our meeting had turned from confrontational to conversational. The man had been testing us at first. Feeling us out. His people had obviously watched our town, listened to our broadcasts, investigated our perimeter, enough to glean an impressive amount of detail relating to who we were, and what we stood for. He might have chosen to go just off of that when encountering us, but he didn't. Face to face was how he operated. He wanted to know any potential friends as well as he did any certain enemies.

"We have somewhere you can sleep tonight after you notify your friends," Dalton said, looking to Hart next. "And if you could look at Moira's wound..."

"Certainly," the medic said.

He and I stood, joining Schiavo and Dalton.

"Thank you," the captain said. "I get to see my husband again because of what you did today."

"It was the right thing to do," Dalton told her.

I imagined that Schiavo knew just how profound a statement that was, particularly in the world as it now existed, a place where wrongs were sometimes necessary to survival, and right could very well be exploited as a weakness.

Except in this man. I doubted that few, if any, had ever used his solid moral compass against him without suffering severe consequence.

"Ansel should be done with the power issue," Dalton told us. "He'll get you to the transmitter and then set you up for the night."

"Thank you," Schiavo said.

"Yes," I concurred with complete sincerity. "Thank you."

Dalton gestured toward the exit to the stairs, extending his hand like a servant might to guide the way. Or like a friend. We stepped through the opening and were about to climb back toward the waning daylight when our host spoke again.

"Eighty-two."

"Pardon," Schiavo said.

"We have eighty two in our community," Dalton elaborated.

"That's a good number to keep alive for so long," I said.

Dalton nodded, but there was a tinge of melancholy about his agreement.

"We started with two hundred and three," he said.

More than half his people gone. Friends, and likely some family as well. He'd suffered and persevered. All these things we'd learned about the man in our very brief time with him made me increasingly comfortable toward our unexpected alliance. And, without much thought on it, I knew why.

Martin.

He reminded me of him. Determined. Fair, firm, protective. We'd been greeted by force when first arriving in Bandon, but that iron fist soon changed to an open hand. We were welcomed after our intentions were confirmed. Here, in Dalton, I saw much the same demeanor and calculation. And I thought it certain that Schiavo must have made note of the very same.

"Your people are lucky to have you," Schiavo said.

Nothing more was said in the basement meeting space. As we climbed the stairs I surveyed the walls, a rough patch job showing over what was likely an even rougher cut through hard earth. They'd dug out this space beneath the building, and there was no doubt that the small room we'd seen was just part of their excavation, which explained much. Our patrols had been spotted, and, like some wily creature, Dalton and his people had retreated to the safety of a manufactured invisibility. That he, and they, had abandoned that defensive posture to intercede in the ambush said much about the level of trust that could develop between our two towns.

We grabbed our weapons and gear from where we'd left them and emerged into the crisp, cool daylight, sun settling toward the western hills. Just up the road, a heavy tow truck rumbled out of a ramshackle building and headed toward the highway, the trio of people visible in the cab giving us a glance as they drove past. In such a wrecker, their only destination could be the site of the ambush to recover our Humvee.

"They don't waste time," Hart said.

I looked around, but Gina was nowhere to be seen. She wasn't guarding the door anymore, nor anything else in view. Still, we were not alone for long as Ansel came around from the back of the building, ducking through a length of chain link peeled back from a rusted fence.

"You all set?"

His question didn't surprise any of us, nor the haste it hinted at. He hadn't been down below when Dalton had promised us radio time and shelter, both which the man before us was supposed to arrange.

"We need to send a message to our town," Schiavo said.

Ansel seemed to puzzle at that, glancing toward the doorway for a second.

"He said you could use the radio?"

"Yeah," I told him. "And he said you had a place for us to bunk tonight until our vehicle is fixed."

The man seemed genuinely, if quietly, surprised. He looked briefly again to the door before nodding at us.

"Then I'll get that done for you," Ansel said. "Follow me."

He started off across the street that paralleled the highway. We followed, Schiavo spotting something as we did.

"Specialist..."

Hart looked and saw her point toward the building from which the tow truck had emerged. Moira was just coming out, shoving the old doors closed over the opening, giving the building a look of abandonment and disrepair. Anyone looking from the outside would hardly think anything of use or value was inside.

"You have a patient," Schiavo said.

"Yes ma'am."

Hart jogged off toward the woman with the wounded shoulder. Ansel eyed the scene sideways, with restrained suspicion. Maybe they were a couple and he felt some jealousy rising. Maybe. But I didn't think so. In fact, I didn't know what to think the man. But I sensed something. Something that wasn't right.

"Radio is up that trail."

Ansel stopped and directed us to a worn path through the grey woods at the base of a hill. The ground was damp from snowmelt, but that would not last long. The sky, clear as it was for most of the day, was darkening with clouds, the temperature dropping as a new front moved in. By morning, when, hopefully, we would be on our way home, the land would be dusted white again.

"When you're done, find me in the back of the old diner," Ansel told us. "There's a place there for the three of you."

Without waiting for an acknowledgment he turned and left us.

"Someone took a leak in his cereal," Schiavo said, judging the man's harsh demeanor toward us. "Or he just doesn't like you."

"It's me," I said.

The captain and I climbed the small hill and made contact with Bandon, Krista answering our call before Westin took over. We gave them a brief rundown of our situation, but Schiavo gave no hint as to the bit of diplomacy she'd engaged in. That would be better done in person, and I was pleased as punch that I would be there to see the reaction of the Defense Council to what she'd arranged.

Twenty One

Night came quick and cold with snow falling just before twelve.

By the time we were ready to turn in, the Humvee had been towed back into town and was pushed into the old garage. Tires for it could be had on the cheap from any number of its brethren that had been abandoned on roads and in fields as efforts to contain lawlessness faltered once the blight had taken hold. The people here would have little difficulty effecting the repairs that had been promised.

Some, though, were not entirely amenable to assisting us.

"Captain," Hart said, sitting on one of the cots that had been provided for us.

"Yes, Trey?" Schiavo asked, the late hour and full day allowing her to address her medic with some informality.

"The woman," Hart said. "Moira. There was something about her."

"I think she's taken," I said, attempting a bit of levity.

But Hart shook his head at that. He was dead serious.

"Her wound was...weird."

Schiavo rolled on her cot and propped herself up on one elbow to face the young soldier.

"How so?"

"It was a laceration, a deep one, really rough. Not from a blade. But when I asked her how it happened she got, I don't know, quiet, and then she gave me a BS answer."

"Why is it BS?" I asked.

"She said it was from falling sheet metal," Hart answered. "That cut wasn't from anything with a clean edge. To me it looked like a jagged piece of wood did the damage. Splintered wood."

"There's enough of that around here," Schiavo said.

She wasn't wrong. Every dead tree, at some point, would fall and splinter. A stumble near one could have sent the woman falling against the ragged hunk of wood.

But Hart didn't think so. He wasn't saying that, but I could tell. He didn't openly doubt his captain's suggestion, but he didn't embrace it either.

"You patched her up, yes?" Schiavo asked.

"Bandaged and antibiotics," Hart confirmed.

"Okay, then her injury is her business."

Schiavo was making it clear that the matter was resolved, at least to her satisfaction. Hart accepted her word and laid back on his cot, settling in for the night, the sound of heavy flakes rustling against the corrugated metal patch job that had been done on the roof.

I knew why Schiavo wasn't keen to entertain any speculation as to the real cause of Moira's wound—propriety. We'd been in Camas Valley all of eight hours after members of their community had saved us from almost certain death. Openly doubting what any of those people said was not even close to the realm of what was acceptable. Particularly after what Schiavo had managed to arrange with Dalton.

Yes, it was odd that Moira would lie, when there was little apparent reason to. But this was their town, and what happened here was their business. That's what I believed.

In the morning as we were about to leave, my opinion would change completely.

Twenty Two

Hart drove the Humvee out of the repair shop and into the falling snow, a good inch on the ground already.

"No plows out there ahead of you," Dalton said as Schiavo and I loaded our gear into the back of the vehicle.

"None needed," the captain said, thumping the hood of the dark green workhorse. "We'll replace the tires you put on from our supply."

"That would be appreciated," Dalton said.

"We'll be in touch as soon as everything is formalized," Schiavo told him.

Dalton reached out and shook her hand again. I took my place in the back, behind Schiavo in the passenger seat. Dalton stepped back from the vehicle, and when he did I could see just past him to where someone stood at the edge of the road. It was Ansel, his face almost unrecognizable through the downpour of white between us.

Wait...

He stood there, looking past his leader, directly at me. Not at the vehicle or the others in it, but at me. Nothing else seemed to hold any interest to him except meeting my gaze. And I suddenly knew why.

Damn...

"Take us home, specialist," Schiavo said, and Hart got us moving.

I didn't look away from Ansel as we drove past, nor he from me. I sensed we both knew what had just happened—recognition.

You could be wrong...

I told myself that. It was a possibility. I was far from infallible.

But here, I wasn't.

"You eager to see your girls, Fletch?"

"I am," I told Schiavo.

There was more I wanted to tell her. Even in light of how she'd handled Hart's doubts toward Moira the night before, what I'd just realized about Ansel could not be withheld. Even if it was just my opinion. An opinion that also related to the woman who'd lied about her injury.

But, what if it wasn't only that? What if there was some evidence? Some fact to back up what I was certain was true? That would take things out of the realm of conjecture.

There was a way. Or there might be. I would know one way or the other once we were back in Bandon.

Twenty Three

I kissed my daughter on the forehead and lowered her into her crib. Elaine stood alongside me and eased a light blanket over our swaddled child. We turned the nightlight on and left Hope to sleep, retiring to the living room.

"Quite the adventure?"

My wife's question was predicated on what she'd heard, not what I'd shared. And I wasn't ready to fill her in on all the details as I saw them. Not yet. Not until I had proof that would support what I believed.

"It was that, and then some."

"Survivors," she said, settling into the couch as I stood near the fire place, the last of a log burning low in the hearth. "I was starting to think we were all that was left. Around here, anyway."

"No," I told her. "We're not alone."

She eyed me for a minute, in that way she did when she sensed something wasn't quite right, her expression both hard and soft at the same time. More worry than wariness in her gaze.

"What's going on?"

"Nothing," I said, mostly lying.

She patted the spot next to her on the couch, signaling for me to join her. But I shook my head.

"I need to do something," I told her.

"What?"

"It'll only take fifteen minutes."

My wife's gaze narrowed down on me.

"Eric, what's going on?"

I took my coat from where I'd earlier draped it over the back of a chair and slipped into it as Elaine's stare shifted to the pistol holstered on my hip.

"You didn't take that off when you got home," she said, realizing what had been obvious since my return just twenty minutes earlier.

"Fifteen minutes, I promise. Then I'll tell you. Everything."

I knew that she trusted me, and my judgment. That didn't mean she preferred being kept in the dark. But I wasn't going to alarm her with possibilities. The truth, supported by facts, was what I needed. And what she deserved.

"Fifteen," she said, allowing a vague smile. "Not sixteen."

I stepped close and leaned down to plant a soft kiss on her warm lips.

"Be right back."

* * *

The absence of snow scraping my face was a welcome change from the night I'd chased the intruder from our house, but I let my mind drift back to that evening as I retraced the steps I'd taken in my pursuit. When I reached the end of my progress, where the masked man had stopped me, I paused. This time, though, I did not retreat to my house to call for reinforcements. This time I continued on.

Enderson, Hart, and Westin had searched for the intruders, and had found items in the snow. A radio. A map. And they had also found a splintered fence post where footprints in the deep snow continued on into the dead woods. I came to that post after walking on a minute longer.

The broken support was obvious, just part of an old picket fence that defined the border of a yard at the very end of the neighboring block. Beyond it there were no more houses. Bandon, as a developed town, ended at this point. I turned my flashlight on and swept the area to my rear. A house, empty, stood there. It was one of many in the town still to be rehabilitated for future occupancy. No one had lived in it since its owner abandoned it and fled for California during the blight.

"No one would see you run through here," I said aloud.

It was a perfect escape route. One that was not stumbled upon by chance. It was planned.

"But you still fell," I said to myself, shifting the light to the jagged end of the fencepost. "Because you'd never been chased before."

I crouched close to the post and examined the rough shards of wood pointing upward. Snow had topped the unbroken support that night, and would have covered it again within an hour after it had been snapped. Rain had drenched it in the interim. There was every likelihood that any evidence left at the moment of impact would be washed away. Gone.

But it wasn't.

"Blood," I said.

There it was. The tawny, fibrous internal structure of the old post was stained a dark color. Black, it appeared, with a tinge of crimson. Someone had been injured right here.

"Moira."

I rose and shined my flashlight into the woods, shades of black and grey defining the darkened landscape. No one out there. Not now. But I had what I needed. Confirmation of a suspicion. Evidence of a lie.

But what to do with it?

* * *

Elaine listened to me lay out everything. When I'd finished, she thought for a moment, considering the possibilities I'd just told her.

"It's forty miles to Camas Valley," she said. "Could they have made it back there without being missed?"

"They have vehicles."

"In the storm that night they'd need them," Elaine said. And who would have followed through the blizzard?

"What do you think?"

There was zero hesitation in my wife's reply.

"You can't keep this to yourself."

"I know," I said.

The only question was when and where to share what I'd learned. With whom was a given.

Part Three

The Alliance

Twenty Four

"They have batteries," Schiavo told the Defense Council, correcting herself for effect. "Let me rephrase that—they are making batteries."

Years ago, in the old world, such a statement would have been greeted with shrugs. But this was not the world of convenience stores with well-stocked shelves, or online retailers where everything from a triple A to a lead acid car battery could be ordered and delivered the next day.

"One of their people is a chemist and worked in the industry," Schiavo said, relaying what Dalton had shared with her to even the scales of the agreement being proposed. "What they produce is crude, but they work. That's according to Dalton."

Mayor Allen, whose connection to the position he held had seemed diminished following the passing of his wife, leaned forward, as if energized by what was being said.

"Batteries," he said, looking to the rest of us.

Us...

That grouping included one who'd missed several meetings recently, for good reason—Elaine. She sat next to me, Martin on her other side. Every few minutes she'd glance instinctively toward the room's door, which was open just a crack. Beyond it, in an office across the hall where a small, folding crib had been set up, Krista sat with our sleeping daughter, her first foray into babysitting. My wife had insisted that she be part of the meeting, something that I could have argued against if it weren't for the fact that there was no reason she shouldn't be. Yes, she was a mother now, with a very small infant to care for, but I'd remembered my father telling stories about his grandmother keeping the farm going after my great grandfather died in a blizzard, leaving her with those forty acres and three young children. Elaine, I knew, was made of the same stuff. Even more so, I knew from experience.

"Martin..."

The town's former leader looked to the man who'd replaced him.

"Yes?"

"What is our supply of batteries?" the mayor asked.

Martin had kept himself involved in the logistics of the town's supply of non-food consumables, be they produced locally or scavenged. Everything from toilet paper to light bulbs to pencils was his purview. Batteries, the life blood of so many necessary electronic devices, large and small, had become a concern of late.

"Shrinking," Martin said. "Patrols have only gathered so many, and a lot of those are nearing expiration if they haven't already failed."

Mayor Allen thought for a moment, this subject very clearly energizing his mind as little had in recent months.

"Batteries," he said again, as if marveling at the possibilities. "We have medical equipment that needs standby power if we lose the grid."

The grid he spoke of was our electrical supply generated by a mix of wind, solar, hydro, and, as a last resort, generator. Continual maintenance had kept the juice flowing almost nonstop, but distribution was another matter.

"The hospital lost power for a brief time during the storm," he said. "Commander Genesee said the generator kicked in, but what if it hadn't? There are monitors and pumps and respirators that could mean the difference between life and death. Not to mention the simple things like flashlights."

Heavy snow and strong winds had snapped a limb from a dead pine and sent it across a field to strike a pair of power lines, plunging the town's only medical facility and surrounding buildings into darkness. The damage was repaired once the weather cleared, but there would be other storms.

"Our portable radios can only recharge so many times," Schiavo said. "The battery packs will have to be replaced eventually. And by eventually I mean soon."

"Those are lithium ion batteries," Elaine said. "Can they manufacture those?"

Schiavo nodded with a hint of lingering surprise.

"Dalton said they can. Lithium ion, nickel cadmium, lead acid, alkaline. It was out of necessity, he said. Their grid isn't as robust as ours."

"We saw that when we were there," I told the Council, recalling the flickering lights that Ansel was sent to deal with.

Ansel...

I had to put him out of my mind for the moment. There would be time to bring him up, but now was not that time, and this was not the place.

"Dalton said they have power issues," Schiavo added. "Plus, they have a repeater we can access to extend our radio range."

That offer, made informally and not part of any trade agreement, would have a positive impact on communications, particularly with distant patrols.

"You believe them," Mayor Allen said, mostly acceptance in the statement. "About the batteries?"

"I do," Schiavo said. "He has no reason to lie. If this is some con, he knows we have the numbers to deal with him."

Mayor Allen mulled that for a moment, then looked to me.

"And you, Fletch...what do you think?"

"I don't believe he's lying," I answered. "We don't know a lot about those around him, though."

From the corner of my eye I saw Schiavo's head angle toward me. I'd expected that reaction. I had no idea how she would respond later when I told her what I knew I had to.

"You have doubts?" Mayor Allen pressed me.

I shook my head, complete truth in the gesture.

"Dalton can be trusted," I said. "And he's the one who matters in Camas Valley. That's very apparent when you see how his people defer to him."

Once more, Mayor Allen thought on what I'd said. On all that had been said.

"We can handle a trade of livestock?" the mayor asked.

"I believe so," Martin answered. "I'll have to check with the farm and ranch crew, but there are a number of pregnant females among the herds. Cows, pigs, goats."

"Chickens aren't an issue," Schiavo added.

"I wouldn't think so," Mayor Allen agreed.

The discussion ended there, and a vote was taken. All were in favor of formalizing the alliance. All that was left to do was work out the details of transfers and improving communications between our communities.

Bandon now had a bona fide ally in the continuing struggle to survive. And to stay free. That was the prevailing wisdom, and I wanted to believe it wholeheartedly. But I couldn't. Not yet.

* * *

Elaine sat on the floor in the office with Krista, both ogling over Hope as she woke from a short nap after the end of our meeting. Schiavo leaned on the wall near the open door and savored the silly, wonderful sight.

"Can I talk to you?" I asked Schiavo.

She seemed puzzled toward my request. At first. Then, without a word said, she gestured toward the side door just outside the conference room, annoyance flourishing where joy had lived just a moment before. When we stood together in the outdoors, with the day's persistent chill wrapping us, Schiavo faced me with a fire in her eyes.

"What is it?"

"It's about Ansel," I said.

She drew a mildly exasperated breath, some tiredness about her.

"Is he the reason you wanted to torpedo this alliance in there?"

"I didn't try to torpedo anything. I was just being honest. I don't think he can be trusted. Or Moira."

"Fletch, we're past this."

"No," I told her. "We're not. He and Moira were the ones who broke into my house."

There was no expression of surprise, or of outrage. She showed no reaction at all to the revelation.

"There was blood on the broken fence picket she and Ansel knocked over getting away," I explained. "And when he looked at me as we drove away, I knew. I recognized his eyes. It was the same as the night he had his weapon in my face, the snow was falling, and we were staring at each other. It was them, Angela. It was. I'm certain of it."

She let that certitude of mine hang there for a moment.

"It doesn't matter, Fletch," she said after the brief silence. "It can't."

"Dalton said they don't steal," I reminded her. "If his top lieutenants are breaking into houses, either he knows or he should."

But to that, she simply glared at me. Disappointed and perturbed all at once.

"Do you know what we might achieve here?" Schiavo challenged me. "Do you?"

I understood much of what was intended with the alliance, but what the captain was asking went beyond the particulars. Whatever answer she wanted me to offer would speak to some motivation. To her motivation.

"Our eastern flank, Fletch. Our entire eastern flank. If we have Camas Valley on board with us, we have more than a tripwire at Remote to warn of any attack. We'll have an honest to goodness fighting force that can repel an aggressor."

She shook her head, seemingly shocked that I didn't recognize the totality of what might come to be.

"I have four shooters, Fletch. Four. If the Unified Government decides to have another go at us, or some wannabe nation state group of survivors picks a fight for the first time, I don't think we can mount a credible defense, even with the citizen volunteers we have. People are tired of fighting."

"But they will fight," I said. "If it comes to that."

"I don't want them to have to," Schiavo countered. "With a solid alliance, we might just be formidable enough to make an adversary think twice before starting something."

She was afraid. I realized that now. Not of a fight, or of putting her life on the line. I'd seen her do so on several occasions. Enough that I knew that lack of bravery was not a fault she harbored. Instead, she was afraid that she would fail in her mission to keep Bandon safe. To keep its people alive. To give the recovery, which had begun here, a chance to flourish.

"We don't need Dalton doubting his own people," she said. "Because if he can't trust them, why should he trust us?"

Her points were valid. I believed mine were as well. But I also knew that the stakes were bigger than my own discomfort with the situation. If this did work, then the alliance Schiavo had crafted almost on the fly would be invaluable to all who had made Bandon their home. And even to those who were soon to leave it.

"You're right," I said, nothing but honesty driving my acquiescence. "This is important."

At that moment, when I'd surrendered to the logic and the plea she'd delivered, her stance toward me softened.

"There are other reasons, Fletch," she said, but expanded on that statement not at all as I waited for her to.

"Reasons you'd rather keep close," I said.

She smiled and nodded.

"Take your wife and baby home, Fletch," Schiavo told me. "Go be a family."

She made her way back into the Town Hall and found her husband. I followed and joined Elaine and Krista, still hovering almost giddily over Hope.

"You ready?" I asked.

Elaine nodded and looked to Krista.

"You want to come home with us or go to the hospital until your mom's done with work?"

"Can I play with Hope?"

"Of course," Elaine said.

Krista did a little shimmy of joy and stood. I crouched and picked up our daughter as Elaine rose from the floor.

"We could pick up Brandon from the sitter and save Grace a trip," my wife suggested.

"He is the destroyer of worlds," Krista said, frowning seriously.

"Sounds fun," Elaine said, looking to me. "How about it? You up for a couple hours of noisy family life?"

"Nothing sounds better," I answered.

"Good," Elaine said. "It will give us a chance to see what having three kids will be like."

She grinned and took Hope from my arms and led Krista out of the office, heading for the side door as I stood there, suddenly slack-jawed, fixing on what my wife had just slyly suggested with one word—*will*.

Twenty Five

His name was Carter. Carter Laws. He was seventeen years, eleven months, and twenty nine days old when he came to Schiavo while she and I were standing outside the garrison's office and told her he wanted to volunteer.

"For what?"

The young man was only briefly taken aback by her question.

"The Army," he said.

Schiavo regarded him first with some surprise, though that reaction very quickly turned on itself as she realized how very normal the young man's statement would have been in the old world.

"We're expanding," Carter said. "Starting a new settlement."

"Yes," Schiavo confirmed.

"There will probably be more," he said.

"Yes."

"Well, if we're growing, don't you think you should, too? The garrison?"

Schiavo smiled at the young man for a moment, then looked to me.

"Does that sound like solid logic to you, Fletch?"

It did. I nodded and gave the young man a quick wink.

"You were saying you only had four shooters the other day," I told Schiavo. "You could make that five."

I could tell by her quiet consideration of the issue that the wheels were already turning in her head as to how she could, and should, make this happen. Not just for Carter, but for any others who wanted to formally serve in the military. The military which she, at the moment, was supreme commander.

Those first thoughts were all logistical and legal. There were more personal issues that would have to be dealt with first.

"You're on your own, Carter, aren't you?"

"I am," he told the captain.

The young man had come to Bandon as a boy just prior to my own arrival, his single mother going missing while out searching for food one night near their Portland neighborhood. After his own dangerous search for her, when it became clear that she wasn't going to return, he set out for Eagle One, following rumors that led him to its location in Bandon. He'd been cared for by locals until, at seventeen, he requested, and was granted, his own place to live, a small apartment near downtown.

"But the town let me live on my own," Carter reminded us, fearing that some reluctance might be creeping into our consideration. "The mayor signed off on it. And, if I can live my own life, shouldn't I be able to serve my country?"

My country...

He was talking, and thinking, like an American. Not just like a resident of a small town on the Oregon coast.

"Easy there, Mr. Laws," Schiavo said. "No one is suggesting you can't do that. I just want to make sure you've, maybe, talked it through with people you know and trust."

"The Langfords, the people who fostered me when I got here, I had a long discussion with them about it. Especially Mr. Langford, since he was a Marine."

"Well, we won't hold that against him," Schiavo commented, grinning as she let the morsel of interservice rivalry fly.

"Pat, Mr. Langford, he kinda said the same thing about you," Carter told her.

It was one of the few times in recent weeks that I'd seen Schiavo relax as she took in the simple banter, which must have reminded her of old times. Of simple times. When finding creative ways to badmouth your fellow service member was elevated to an art form.

"You know, I'm going to talk to Sergeant Lorenzen about this," Schiavo said. "I think he'd be the best person to figure out how to go about making this happen."

Carter beamed at the positive words.

"You mean I'm in?"

"Barring any complications, health issues..."

"Nothing," Carter said emphatically. "I'm totally healthy. I don't even get colds."

"That's good to know," Schiavo said, smiling as she offered the young man her hand. "We'll be in touch."

He accepted the gesture, shaking the captain's hand before turning and running, leaping into the air with joy when he was halfway down the block.

"You're going to need a recruiting office," I said.

"We should be so lucky," Schiavo replied, looking to me once the soldier-in-waiting was gone from sight. "Thanks for stopping by."

Westin had called the house on Schiavo's behalf, asking if I could stop by. With all the preparations for the settler's move to Remote, there was much to be done. I'd been helping with gathering tools, drafting plans, and listing where items required to make the necessary repairs in Remote could be scavenged.

"What is it?"

"Corporal Enderson is going to be joining Hart to staff the Remote outpost," she said. "He volunteered as soon as he heard the plan."

"He's a good man," I said. "They all are."

"I need Westin here for com, and the sergeant, well, he's going to be busier than he has been," she said, referencing the obvious training regimen Lorenzen would have to come up with for Carter Laws. "But..."

I waited through her hesitation, though I probably should have expected what she finally asked when she spoke.

"Would you consider going to Remote to get the repairs on track?"

The reason for her hesitation was clear now. Others she could order to do what needed to be done, even though they would offer themselves up as volunteers before the issue was forced. I was a civilian. My life was my own. And my life was here. With my family.

"Angela..."

"I know, I know," she said, true apology and reluctance in her words. "But they're not ready and the move starts in two days. I've been talking almost non-stop with Mike and Rebecca, and they just don't have the skillset among the people going with them to handle what needs to be done."

Schiavo wasn't asking me to take a short trip with her to inspect the town. That had already been done. The request she'd just made would require a week's stay or more.

More...

All that needed to be done in the tiny hamlet ticked off in my head. The list was almost daunting. Roofs, walls, plumbing. A septic system would have to be redone, with excavation of a new leach field to handle waste water from the newly inhabited dwellings. Solar arrays and generators would have to be installed and connected to a very localized power grid. Until all these things happened, the settlers who were going to call Remote home would be living in less than satisfactory conditions.

In all those items I'd just listed, the reason why Schiavo had asked me what she had became clear. As did the many reasons why I had to say yes.

Except, I couldn't. Not yet.

"I can't give you an answer," I said.

Schiavo nodded, both understanding and hope in her reaction.

"I have to talk to Elaine," I said.

"Yes," Schiavo said. "You do."

Twenty Six

Elaine was not as receptive this time to the idea of me being away. Particularly for the amount of time that would be required.

Other considerations, though, informed her resistance to the extended assignment.

"And what about the people you told me about? The ones who broke in here? Being in Remote would put you in direct contact with them."

"Not necessarily," I said.

"Can you promise that?"

I couldn't.

"I don't know why they did what they did," I said. "There's no reason for them to target us."

"What about just you?"

I'd told her what Martin had thought about the other break-ins being diversionary. And I'd shared with her what I'd found in Remote, incontrovertible evidence of Olin's presence at some point. She had all the pieces to speculate just as I had as to the reason for any special focus on me.

"If Olin is there..." she said.

"These are two separate things," I reminded her, recalling Schiavo's words when I'd shown her the rocks left by the man who murdered my friend. "He probably passed through there on his way east, heading back to where he came from."

"So Martin is wrong? And what you saw doesn't matter?"

"No," I told her, pacing across the living room floor, away from where she stood near the front door, dusk tipping toward night just beyond. "This is all just bigger than fears, all right? We're trying to accomplish something here."

"That's Angela talking," Elaine said.

I stopped and faced her. Her arms were drawn tight across her chest, a look of mild anger and raging fear about her. There was nothing I could say to convince her that this was even close to a good idea, even if what the evidence suggested was unfounded. In the end, I decided to say nothing, and grabbed my coat from the closet and walked past her, onto the porch and down the walkway. As I reached the sidewalk, the front door slammed behind me.

* * *

We'd had disagreements, but nothing I would have termed a fight. Until now.

I walked down our block and followed a path that would take me to the coast as it meandered through an orchard which had been planted near the south side of town. The pear trees were naked, their limbs fully bare since late autumn. Nearly full, the moon above cast twisted shadows from the gangly branches that would bear fruit in spring and summer. There was enough confidence now to believe that the trees and fields would again bloom and sprout and provide Bandon with the bounty it needed.

There were times, though, when such confidence came second to what my friend had espoused so plainly—hope. As a town we still embraced the ideal of that. As a man, it had become the thing that drove me. Hope for a better future for my child. And for my wife.

She was rightfully upset at the possibility I'd brought into our home. Absence, my absence, would introduce fear into our home. Into our relationship. She would fear for me, and I would fear...

"For her."

This was a two way street, I realized as I reached the shore. That, though, did not negate the necessity of what had to be done. Of what *I* had to do.

I walked on the beach, thinking. Trying to find some solution. Waves crashed to my right, the moonlight painting the foaming surf a ghostly white. It also highlighted in silhouette a man standing on the low bluffs to my left.

I stopped and fixed on the figure, less than a hundred feet from me. We were just beyond the southernmost part of town, the last of the inhabited houses a few hundred yards to the north. Two of us had, apparently, decided to take a stroll in the moonlight. But who was my unknown companion? I had no idea. Just some fellow resident of Bandon whose identity was lost in shadow.

"Hello!"

My greeting easily carried the distance between us, and the hand I raised and waved would be perfectly visible in the bright light of the moon. There was no way the man could miss either.

But he did not call out to me with a greeting of his own. He did not wave. He made no move, in fact, until one of his hands came up and placed a cowboy hat upon his head.

Olin...

There was nothing more than that image in silhouette to indicate that the shadowy figure a third of a football field away was him. I could not see his face, nor any telling features. Only that hat.

In my gut, though, I felt him. Standing there. Staring down at me from the bluffs.

"Olin!"

I shouted at the man and put my hand on my holstered Springfield. He still made no move. Gave no reaction at all. His blacked-out form simply stood there, facing me, until he turned without a word and began to walk away.

"OLIN!"

This time I nearly screamed his name as I took off running, reaching the base of the bluffs as he disappeared beyond the rim above. I scrambled up the damp slope, clawing with my hands and digging with my feet, finding purchase wherever I could, climbing higher, and higher, and higher. Finally I reached the top and bolted onto flat earth.

But he was nowhere to be seen.

I drew my pistol and took a ready stance, sweeping left and right. The only place he could have found cover was in an old, leaning shack between the bluffs and the woods beyond. There was no way he could have made it into the thick stand of dead pine. Not without me seeing him.

It had to be the shack.

The muzzle of my Springfield stayed locked on the small building as I approached it, each step slow and deliberate. At one time the structure had housed a tiny shop which sold drinks and candies to tourists who came to walk along the picturesque shore. Or so I'd been told. As long as I'd been in Bandon, the teetering shack had seemed ready to fall, and clearly almost had in the recent blizzard. But for now it stood, harboring the man who'd murdered my friend.

An opening where a window had once been came into view, not a sliver of glass remaining in its frame. I eased close to it and paused, listening. For movement. Breathing. For anything.

But I heard nothing.

I crouched and moved below the level of the window, staying out of sight to anyone within, coming to the front corner of the dilapidated structure. My weapon low and ready, I moved quickly around the corner, light of the moon bathing the front of the building with a harsh, ashen light which revealed the entrance. It was nothing more than a space where a door once hung. Blackness lay beyond its threshold. That and the man I'd pursued here.

With my off hand I retrieved the small flashlight I always carried from my pocket and pressed its lens against my coat before switching it on, keeping the beam hidden as I approached the door. I was ready. The plan was to step fast through the doorway, both light and weapon coming up at the same instant to sweep the interior and find my target, keeping in mind that there very well could be return fire. Almost certainly would be, I corrected myself.

That didn't matter. I was not going to pass an opportunity, maybe the only one I would have, to end the man who'd killed Neil. I had him cornered. Leaving to bring reinforcements would only allow him the chance to slip away. Why he'd come back was something I might never know, and I didn't particularly care. This was a confrontation, a reckoning, that had to happen.

I gave myself no count. The time simply came, I drew a breath, and made my move, spinning away from the exterior wall and through the doorway, finger on the trigger, beam of my flashlight arcing across the cramped interior.

The cramped, empty interior.

There was nothing. And no one. Not a stick of old furniture. No broken pieces of a chair or table. And no Tyler Olin.

I killed my light and stepped back outside, trying to make sense of what I'd just seen. And what I hadn't. The only other cover besides the old shack were the dead woods, another seventy yards in the distance. There was no way the man could have made it that distance before I reached the top of the bluff. No chance. I would have seen him.

Would I have?

The sudden doubt was not limited to any estimation I'd made about Olin's ability to cover some arbitrary distance. It extended to the very encounter itself.

He was there, I told myself with waning conviction. *Right?*

There'd been a man atop the bluffs. A man who'd donned a cowboy hat. A figure in silhouette who looked like Olin.

A shadow...

I wondered, suddenly, if the man I'd seen had been just that—a shadow in my mind.

"Dear God, what's happening to me?"

Something was wrong. Something had been wrong for a while. That realization raged now, setting my head to spin and my knees to go wobbly.

I crouched down, the Springfield dangling in my grip until I let it slip to the ground, my own body settling further until I was sitting on the damp earth outside the shack. My face tipped toward the moon and I began to weep.

Twenty Seven

The leader of our town switched on the porch light and opened the front door to find me standing just outside.

"Fletch…"

"Doc, I…"

When my hesitation lingered the elderly man pushed the screen door outward and stepped out onto the porch, robe and pajamas covering his wiry frame. He seemed almost too thin, too frail, but I'd chosen to come to him. I'd run, in fact, from the bluffs to his door, standing outside in the chill for a full five minutes to catch my breath before knocking and waking him. All because I was terrified.

"I think I may be losing it."

Doc Allen put a hand gently upon my shoulder and tipped his head toward the door.

"Come on in and let's talk."

* * *

Doc Allen hung up the phone and joined me in his kitchen, taking a seat at the small table. He'd made a pot of coffee and poured me a cup.

"Elaine is fine," he told me. "I just let her know you stopped by here."

"This is going to be fun to explain to her," I said.

"Why don't you fill me in first?"

I spent the next ten minutes doing just that. Everything from spotting rocks used by Olin in a building in Remote, to what I saw on the bluffs just a thirty minutes earlier—or what I thought I'd seen. For good measure I threw in the suspicions I had about Ansel and Moira, hoping to complete the picture of paranoia even I was beginning to see in myself.

"Am I cracking up?"

The old doctor smiled lightly and shook his head.

"I'm not trained as a psychiatrist, Fletch. But I've come across hundreds of people in my years of practicing medicine who believed that they were going crazy. Not a one of them was."

"Then what is this?" I pressed him.

He considered the question for a moment

"I think it's a few things. Stress from the responsibility you feel to this town, and now also to your growing family. Fear, a righteous fear, because your house was broken into. And grief."

"Grief about Neil," I said, cluing in on where he was going with his analysis.

"You couldn't save him, so you obsess over the man who killed him, both consciously and subconsciously. Those feelings inform all the other things you have to deal with. The new settlement. The intruders. Everything to you right now is magnified tenfold."

"All because of Neil," I said.

Doc Allen reached across the table and put a hand atop mine.

"Fletch, he betrayed you by lying to you, and then he up and got himself killed before you could work that out together. For you, he's still dying."

I nodded, both relieved and ashamed at the same time. Doc Allen eased his hand off mine and sat back in the chair, his gaze settling on the table, fixed on a spot right before me.

"I still talk to her," the man said. "Every morning. She doesn't answer, but I wish she would."

He was speaking of his wife. His Carol. The virus released by the Unified Government had taken her, but had not, and could not, wipe her memory away. That was mostly a blessing.

"Her coffee cup would sit right there," Doc Allen told me, gesturing to a spot near where my hand lay on the small kitchen table. "Mine was right here. We'd drink, and talk, every morning. Sometimes every night."

The old doctor quieted for a moment, looking off toward the darkness in the hall beyond the kitchen.

"I think if I let myself, Fletch, I could see her, maybe standing in that doorway, smiling at me. That would be nice. But it wouldn't be real."

"You think I didn't see him," I said. "That I let my mind make him up."

"I don't know who, or what, you saw, or didn't see. I do know that you have to start letting yourself off the hook. You couldn't have prevented what happened. Neither could Neil."

The doctor was right. But I still viewed myself harshly for allowing the person my mind had almost certainly conjured on the bluffs be the man who killed my friend, and not my friend himself.

"I don't know how to do that," I said.

"You don't have to figure it out," he told me. "Not on your own. Because you're not alone. Someone else is invested in you figuring this out. Two someones, actually."

Elaine. And Hope. They were my reasons for living. And more.

"You might just find the answers with them," Doc Allen said.

* * *

I thanked the doc and walked home in the moonlit darkness. My wife was waiting for me when I came through the front door.

"I'm sorry," she said.

"I'm more sorry," I told her.

The half mile I'd covered from Doc Allen's hadn't passed without rumination. I'd thought on what the wise man had told me, but mostly about one possible cause of my distress that he'd mentioned—fear.

He wasn't wrong, but one aspect of that emotion he'd missed. And I was looking at her right now.

"I was thinking," I began, but she did not let me finish.

"You have to go," Elaine said, and for an instant my heart skipped a beat before I realized that some greater divide had not opened between us. "You're going to be needed in Remote."

"So are you," I said.

She quieted, her gaze narrowing down on me.

"Remote doesn't need me."

"No," I said. "But I do. And I will, especially when I'm there."

Once again, she regarded me through a silence that lingered as she tried to understand the 'why' of what I was saying.

"If you're here, you and Hope, half of my thoughts will be about you. And a hundred percent of my worry. I can't function like that. At least not right now."

"What happened, Eric? While you were with the doc?"

"Some things that weren't apparent to me got a little more apparent," I said.

"That's as clear as mud," Elaine told me, with honesty that was anything but unclear.

I stepped close and took her hands. Behind, down the hallway, our daughter made the kind of sound we'd gotten used to hearing while she slept. Reassuring little cooing that warmed our hearts.

"I can't go without you," I said.

She squeezed my hands and looked at me with eyes that were filled with both love and her own concern.

"Of course we'll go with you," she said. "There's no question about that. But..."

She wanted to press, I could tell. To dig out of me what I'd talked with Doc Allen about. And I would open up to her if she asked, sharing my fear that Neil's death was still weighing on me, in disturbing ways.

But she did not pry anymore. I did not have to tell her that there was every chance I'd imagined seeing Olin on the bluffs. That I'd chased a shadow with my weapon in hand. The murderer of my friend, I didn't have to share, was not only invading my dreams, but appearing in my waking world.

"We're a family," she said, wrapping her arms around me and pulling herself tight against my chest. "We should be together. No matter what."

No matter what...

I held my wife and thought on those words. There was commitment in them, but there was also risk. The risk that she, and Hope, would be with me if something went wrong.

But nothing was going to go wrong. We were going to go to Remote, I was going to do my job, and we would return home to Bandon. The fears I'd let get under my skin had been both natural and irrational. I was moving beyond them. Moving forward. The past was not my future.

Not if I could help it.

Twenty Eight

The convoy pulled out of Bandon early on a Thursday under a steely sky that spat showers at the short train of vehicles heading inland. Three of the heavy trucks which had been left during one of the *Rushmore*'s supply visits, along with a Humvee, made up the bulk of the train of vehicles, with a few pickups and sedans filling out the parade rumbling out of town. Friends and neighbors of those striking out stood along the roads, waving and smiling, wishing these new pioneers good luck.

They would need that luck. But I believed they had amongst them something more important—determination. And I didn't mean just the desire to get things done. No, it was more the act of determining their purpose. Their present. The destiny they sought collectively. The decisiveness they'd exhibited in their meeting with me, and in the preparations for the move, was nothing short of admirable. Here were people taking on the very act of survival, leaving behind a support system that was there at a moment's notice, which would now be more than an hour away.

I didn't agree with everything they had expressed, nor fully with what they were doing, but they had earned my respect, and I wanted to help them have the best shot at succeeding.

"Hope's first road trip," Elaine said, holding our daughter in the passenger seat of our pickup.

"When she's a little more mobile we should take her to the cottage on the coast," I said.

There were painful memories there, at the place from which I'd been snatched during a getaway with Elaine. But I'd moved past that, and it was such a beautiful spot south of Bandon. Beautiful and peaceful. Being there, with Elaine, with Hope, listening to waves crash with a fire in the hearth, would be a slice of heaven on earth.

"That sounds amazing," Elaine said.

Just ahead, standing at the curve, Grace stood, Krista at her side, the growing girl holding her beefy brother. I pulled to the side, letting the tail end of the convoy pass me. Elaine rolled down the window and reached a hand out, our friend taking it and smiling through a sheen of tears.

"It's just a couple weeks," Elaine said.

"I know," Grace said, reaching with her free hand to wipe her eyes. "It's just..."

"What?" I probed, leaning toward the passenger window.

"You're the people I know best," she said. "You're the ones I missed most when we were gone."

I understood. When she and Neil and Krista had boarded the chopper to be spirited away from Bandon, her worry was obvious. She trusted her husband, but she was still leaving those who'd supported her, and who would continue to do so as she carried the child that grew inside her at that time. Now, that bruiser of a boy squirmed in his big sister's arms, pulling at her hair as she blew raspberries at his giggling face.

"We're going to need you to sit with Hope again when we get back," Elaine told Krista.

"Really?"

The girl looked up to her mother, who rescued her from being mauled by her sibling and lifted Brandon to a one armed hold on her hip.

"Can I?" Krista asked, just shy of begging. "Please?"

Grace had let her daughter, less than a year shy of being a full-fledged teenager, watch over Hope across from the Defense Council's meeting a just two weeks earlier. That allowance was made due to the proximity of both mother and father. Any near term sitting for us, Grace knew, would fall under similar circumstances, with Elaine and me in the backyard doing work, or enjoying an evening together on the porch. There would come a time when we would actually venture away from the house while someone sat with our child, so grooming Krista was an act of preparation, in addition to giving the sweet girl something to do beyond her schoolwork and duties working Micah's transmitters.

"Of course," Grace said.

Krista reached out and stole Elaine's hand from her mother.

"I promise I'll do a good job," she said, sincere enthusiasm all about her.

"We know that, sweetie," I said. "But we're going to have to figure out some way to pay you."

The days of money were over—for now. There had been discussions of how to introduce some currency into what had become a very fluid barter system. That was a decision, and an effort, I wanted nothing to do with.

"But we can figure that out later," I told the girl.

She let go of Elaine's hand and stepped close to her mother and brother.

"I've got to get Brandon to Mrs. Detwiler's so I can get to work," Grace said.

My friend's widow had arranged for a trio of older women to care for her son while she worked at the town's hospital, which, until recently, most had been referred to as a clinic. It had become more than that by necessity. A place where bones were set, cuts were stitched, tumors were removed, and children were born, the facility provided every possible care that Commander Genesee and, when needed, Doc Allen were capable of.

"We'll see you in a couple weeks," I said through the window. "Take care."

Grace and Krista gave us a wave as I pulled away, accelerating to join the back end of the convoy. In a few minutes the line of vehicles was out of town, cruising slowly along Highway 42 as the rain that had been falling eased, clouds parting ahead to the east, enough that long rays of sunlight pierced the storm and spread across the sky, glowing and translucent.

"All these people," Elaine said, looking to the trucks and vehicles ahead. "They're pioneers."

"I hope they find what they want," I commented.

Elaine nodded. I glanced to her and noticed that the Mp5 which had been on the floor of the pickup, lying at her feet, was now on her lap, one hand resting atop the grip. And as we entered the deeper woods, grey trees sweating a dewy dust in the damp morning air, I sensed her head swiveling, scanning to either side of our vehicle. I might have thought the action a throwback to her days as an FBI agent, just a cop's vigilance on display. But most who'd survived this long through the blight had developed a similar sense of awareness to their surroundings. It didn't trouble me that she was on guard. That was who she was.

But it did remind me that there could be any number of threats out there. The hiders Dalton had spoken of, like those who'd ambushed us, could be behind any tree. Whether they were willing to take on a convoy of this size was debatable. But we had to be ready. My wife knew that.

It was a shame that, almost certainly, my daughter would have to be taught the same lessons as she grew older.

Twenty Nine

Our quarters were temporary, a house a hundred yards north of the covered bridge. Once we'd unloaded the pickup and received our supplies from the larger trucks in the convoy, Elaine and I set up Hope's collapsible crib and laid her in it. Her eyes swept the unfamiliar space above, hands groping free of the blanket which wrapped her.

"She's so active now," Elaine said. "When she's feeding she's grabbing at my face, my hair."

I looked around the front room of the house which we'd been assigned during our stay in Remote. A beadboard panel had peeled away from the underlying two-by-four structure. Above, the plastered ceiling had cracked and a four foot section lay in the corner of the space.

"Maybe we can give her a hammer and she can help get this place together," I said.

Elaine, too, gave the room a once over.

"It's not so bad," she said.

"It's not so great, either."

"We've stayed in worse," she reminded me.

How true that was. In little more than collapsing shacks and outdoors on our way to and from Cheyenne. In the belly of a fishing boat chugging north to Alaska.

"Besides," she began, "we're together. All of us. That's what's important."

I leaned close and kissed her. Below us, our daughter made a sound that almost reeked of amusement.

"Was that a laugh?" Elaine asked, both of us staring at Hope.

"You need some manners, young lady," I said, pulling Elaine into an embrace and kissing her deeply.

Again, our daughter chuckled. This time, though, neither of us let the other go. The moment, regardless of the locale, felt too wonderful to stop.

* * *

We met at the garrison's outpost in the converted general store. Enderson and Hart had set up half a dozen chairs, but only five were needed.

"Nick is wrangling an uncooperative generator," Mike DeSantis explained.

A top notch mechanic, Nick Withers had fought alongside me against the Unified Government forces. That encounter, I'd feared, had broken him. But it hadn't. He'd recovered from the episode where fear had frozen him, and was pulling more than his own weight in the establishment of the settlement.

"We'll fill him in on what we discuss," Rebecca Vance said.

She took a seat, Mike next to her, notebook open on his lap where a computer tablet would have been not so many years before. The two soldiers and I joined them in the rough circle of chairs.

"Our first night," Corporal Enderson said. "We don't expect any problems or threats, but everyone should stay aware. If something serious does develop, two shots in rapid succession will let me and Specialist Hart know that we're needed. And that's our plan—to back you up if necessary. This is your town."

Mike smiled and nodded at the simple explanation of the garrison's role in Remote. Rebecca, though, held any reaction close, her deep suspicions seeming to not allow even the slightest approval of actions authorized by Bandon's leadership.

"Fletch is here to assist with the repairs and construction," Enderson continued. "I know he's discussed plans with you."

"He has," Mike confirmed. "It's an aggressive schedule, but I think we can manage it and wrap things up in two weeks."

"Good," Enderson said. "So then if—"

"What about these people to the east?" Rebecca asked, interrupting. "These people *you've* made an alliance with."

"Camas Valley," Enderson said.

"What do they expect from us?"

"Nothing," I said, answering for the corporal. "The arrangements are between Bandon and them."

"And we're in the middle," Rebecca stated.

She wasn't entirely incorrect. But not for the reasons she thought.

"Rebecca, once the garrison outpost is gone, and it will be gone eventually, if you all of a sudden need the cavalry, Camas Valley is a lot closer than Bandon," I said. "Not everyone is out to oppress you."

I might have held back, but, since I was the first person to be on the receiving end of Rebecca's distrust when she and Nick and Mike came to my house, I figured I'd heard enough of her complaining, warranted or not. But the reaction I received from her, to my surprise, was not some volley of vitriolic return fire.

"We just don't know them," she said.

"Trust is an issue, Fletch," Mike said, joining with his fellow settler. "We'd like to meet them at some point."

"I'm sure that will happen sooner rather than later," Enderson said, looking to Hart next. "Specialist..."

"Any medical issues, injuries, anything like that, let me know right away," Hart said. "I'd like to prevent any—"

The medic's encouragement to bring issues quickly to his attention ended abruptly as the building began to shake, the structure rolling through a sizeable earthquake. I stood, the floor beneath my feet shifting enough that I reached out to the old counter to steady myself.

"It's settling down," Enderson said as the motion slowed, the world stilling around us.

"That was interesting," Mike said.

I looked to the door, wanting to bolt through it and get to my wife and daughter. But I didn't. The shaker hadn't been violent enough to do any appreciable damage, so they would certainly be safe, particularly with Elaine watching over our daughter.

"A damage survey would seem appropriate," Enderson said. "Fletch?"

"I wouldn't expect much from this one," I said. "But we don't want to start off repairing new damage tomorrow if we can deal with it tonight."

"Let's touch base tomorrow to see if we have any issues crop up after the workday," Enderson suggested.

"Agreed," Mike said.

The meeting, as formally informal as a gathering such as this could be, broke up, each of us not wearing a uniform heading back to their homes to give the structures a quick once over after the quake.

Rebecca, though, did not go straight home.

I was last to leave, talking with Enderson and Hart for just a minute. When I finally came through the front door and stood in the shelter of the outpost's covered drive, where automobiles had once pulled in for gas, I saw Rebecca standing near one of the posts supporting the horizontal structure. She'd leaned her AK against the post and was lashing a length of wood to the support so that it jutted upward at an angle, as a short pole might.

And that was just what it was, I realized. A pole. A flag pole. That became abundantly clear when she reached into her backpack and retrieved the bolt of cloth, stars and stripes upon it. She tied Old Glory to the pole and stepped back, letting the breeze catch it and smooth the folds.

"It looks nice," I said.

The woman turned toward me, not surprised by either my presence or my comment.

"I brought it just in case," she said. "And the place didn't look right without it."

I'd been assured by the leaders of the settlers that they would still consider themselves part of the United States of America, even if they'd separated from Bandon. Rebecca Vance had taken it upon herself to demonstrate that very fact in the truest way possible.

"No, it didn't," I agreed.

* * *

I returned home to find a fire crackling in the hearth and a broken window I'd planned to deal with in the morning already boarded over.

"You've been busy," I said as I came into the kitchen.

"Just don't get used to this domestic side of me," Elaine admonished me.

There would be no cooking with electricity in this kitchen. Not yet. I had seen when coming in that Elaine had rigged up one of the fireplace pokers to hold the Dutch oven we'd brought with us over the fire in the hearth.

"We're cooking old school tonight," she said. "And tomorrow night. And..."

"The night after that," I joined in. "Etcetera."

I gave the space a quick once over and took a step toward the hallway.

"Nothing broken," Elaine said. "No new cracks."

I stopped and smiled at my wife as she dumped chicken pieces into the pot already brimming with beans and tomatoes.

"You're a qualified inspector now," I said.

She put a lid on the heavy pot and handed it to me.

"Go cook us some chili. I'm going to check on Hope."

I did as I was told, hooking the pot's handle to the poker before easing it over the fire. The contents began to sizzle almost immediately. But my attention was drawn away by my wife's voice, uncertainty in it.

"Eric..."

I turned toward her. She stood where the hallway spilled into the front room, her gaze fixed out a side window that looked into the woods.

"Who is that woman?"

I stood and looked out the same window and saw immediately who had drawn my wife's attention. It was a woman, standing deep amongst the trees, most of her lost in shadow. But not her hair, enough fading daylight left to hint at the long red locks draped over her shoulders.

"She's not one of ours," I said, stepping toward the door and taking my AR in hand. "Watch my back."

Elaine retrieved her MP5 and stood near the window as I stepped outside and came around the porch. By the time I reached the side the woman was on, she was gone. I looked back to Elaine and saw her gesturing through the window, pointing up the slope. I redirected my attention and saw movement, quick movement, the figure almost lost in the thickening forest. Had Elaine not seen what I was, I might have thought I was hallucinating, seeing yet another shadowy figure that fled before I could reach it. But this was real. The woman out there was real.

I aimed myself at the place the woman had last slipped through the trees, pushing myself up the gentle hill. Too fast, it turned out, an old, dried out root jutting up from near the base of one tree catching my foot, sending me stumbling forward. Regaining my footing, I pressed on. But on toward nothing. There was no more target to aim myself at.

The woman was gone.

Thirty

Nick Withers and I brought my pickup to the large storage building next to the outpost to peel some clapboards from the side and metal panels from the roof. In a few days the structure would be scavenged down to bare bones, which would then be cut up for firewood.

"What are those people called?" Nick asked me as we stepped from my pickup. "Hiders?"

"That's what Dalton called them."

"Maybe the woman was one of them," Nick suggested.

I'd reported the encounter Elaine and I had had with the woman the previous evening, and it had spread quickly through the new residents of Remote. No one else had seen her, it turned out, nor noticed any sign of a visitor.

"It's possible," I said.

"What about someone from Camas Valley?"

"Just out for a look at us?" I asked.

"Isn't that what they did to everyone in Bandon? Spy on us?"

If that was the case, this woman was the least covert observer I'd ever seen. But, I had to admit, when I'd first laid eyes on her, right after Elaine had pointed her out, it did appear that she was watching us. The collective us, I reminded myself. Even though...

Even though she was near our house, and no others.

I forced that burst of paranoia down and came around the front of the truck, gesturing to the building.

"We've got work to do," I said.

Nick and I each took hold of the twisted front door and peeled it fully back, separating it from the overhead track upon which it had once rolled freely.

"So do you think she was spying?" Nick pressed.

The man was strong in the physical sense, but a tad weak upstairs. Rumor and gossip fed him, I was learning.

"Nick, it really doesn't matter," I told him as we laid the remnants of the door away from the entrance. "If she comes back, we can ask her."

He seemed to take my statement as a signal that I was tired of the subject, which I was.

"I'll get the ladder," he said.

The plan was simple—we'd start at the top, Nick on top of the building to pry the edges of the metal roofing loose, while I'd pound it upward from below using a length of two-by-four. It only took a few minutes for the young mechanic to place the ladder and climb up, demolition bar in hand.

"I'll be right under you inside," I said. "Give me a shout when you have one edge loose and I'll start pounding."

"Got it."

I carried the two-by into the storage building and positioned myself below where Nick was standing. He loosened the first panel and I bashed it free of its remaining fasteners from below. With a few pulls he dislodged the slab of thin metal and tossed it to the ground below, shifting his position to the next panel and setting to work on it. Two were removed. Then three. Then four.

At five the effort stopped cold.

"Fletch..."

The young man called to me through the opening above, but I did not answer. I couldn't. My attention was fixed not on the roof we were dismantling, but on the ground just beyond my feet.

It was the spot I'd stumbled upon when surveying the building on our inspection trip to Remote. Schiavo had come in and found me doing almost the exact same thing I was doing now—staring at two small rocks which had been arranged next to each other in the same fashion as Olin had at his hideout. He'd used them to cook over there, and it seemed as though he must have here, as well, with Schiavo stating that he must have done so on his way to Bandon, or while fleeing.

But how could I be staring at them as I was? I'd knocked them away with a kick of my boot before the captain and I had left the building.

I had done that, I was certain. Or was I?

Could that be just a phantom memory? An innocuous belief that I actually had scattered the pair of angular stones?

"You did," I said to myself, confirming the impossible.

"Fletch, you okay?"

I looked behind and through the growing rectangular hole in the roof. Nick Withers stood at the edge of the opening, squinting down into the darkness at me.

"Anything wrong?"

I shook my head. What was I going to say to him? To anybody? That rocks that shouldn't be here were?

"Nothing," I told Nick. "Just taking a breather."

"Mind if I take one?"

"Not at all," I told him.

I listened to his footsteps on the roof as he moved toward the ladder. I turned back to the stones, staring at them for a few seconds before stepping close and swiping my boot across the dusty floor, knocking them against the wall and into a pile of debris.

Again.

* * *

Elaine had begun tending to the outside of our house, which would become a settler's place of residence once we departed. I found her on the side of the building, Glock on her hip, applying a bead of glazing putty to a cracked but usable window pane. Beyond it was our daughter's room, and every few seconds as she worked I could see my wife peering through, checking on the most precious thing either of us had ever known.

"You're beautiful," I said.

My compliment startled her. She turned abruptly, catching her breath before smiling at me.

"You could have not come up like a ninja," she chided me.

I nodded, but did not approach her. Instead, I stood back, trying to hold it together, my obvious attempt to retain my composure impossible for her to miss.

"Eric, what is it?"

She put her tools down and came to where I stood a few yards away. She put a hand to my face and looked past me to the driveway. The empty driveway.

"Where's the pickup?"

"Nick is loading roofing panels into it," I told her.

"You walked back here," she said.

"I had to. I needed...to think. And now I need to talk."

She led me to the porch and we sat on the steps, door open behind so we could hear our daughter within. I told her about my visit with Doc Allen, which she'd wanted to know about, but hadn't pried. I told her about the man I'd seen on the bluffs, or hadn't seen. And then I told her what I'd just seen in the storage building next to the outpost.

"Either I'm losing it, Elaine, or..."

She squeezed my hand and shook her head.

"You're not losing it," she said.

They were words of comfort. And they were more than that. There was something behind the statement. Some knowing, or some suspicion. This I knew as her gaze ticked off me after she'd spoke the assurance.

"What is it?" I asked.

She refocused on me and seemed to gather her thoughts for a moment before answering.

"There was a technique we would use in the Bureau," she began, harkening back to her time as an FBI agent, "we called it 'tripping'."

"Tripping?"

"Yeah," she said. "And contrary to the name, it didn't involve drugs."

"What was it?"

"It was...subtle," she said. "Most of the time. You would do things to get a suspect to doubt themselves. To believe they were making mistakes, or had made mistakes. Trip them up, hence the name."

I understood, but I wasn't following.

"Why?"

"Let's say you have a suspect who you have under surveillance," she explained. "You know they've hidden documents, embezzled funds, it doesn't matter."

"This is white collar crime," I said.

"Exactly. These are usually smart people who aren't career criminals. So if you introduce doubt into their lives, they begin to question their actions. Especially concerning things they don't usually do."

"Like commit crimes," I said, the first outlines of what she was describing taking shape.

"A lot of times this was all it would take to make them revisit what they'd done to hide their crime," Elaine said. "And with them under surveillance, we would have everything. Location, account numbers, everything."

With a wave of clarity rushing over me, I knew exactly what she was suggesting.

"Or where they hid a deadly biological agent," I said.

"Olin is a field operative, if what he described to you was true, and I think we have to assume it was. He would have been trained in these same techniques to use on adversaries, or on people with intelligence that the Agency needed."

"You think he was doing this to me."

She shook her head.

"No, I think he still is."

The sight of him on the bluffs, the rocks. If he was responsible for those things, those efforts to trip me up, then that meant only one thing of consequence.

"He's still here."

Elaine agreed with a nod. I let out a very slow breath, some weight suddenly gone from my being.

"It feels good to know that I'm not a head case."

"I can imagine," Elaine said, gripping my hand more tightly now than just a moment before. "You can't go after him."

I hadn't said anything of the sort. But I didn't have to.

"I know you want to," she said. "You can't. You have to let this play out."

"Play out?"

"Let him run his op to trip you up, but don't ultimately bite."

"I couldn't if I wanted to."

The location of the sample of BA-412 had gone to the grave with Neil, whose murderer, with that act, had made a successful completion of his mission virtually impossible to achieve.

"He doesn't know that," Elaine said, stating the obvious. "As long as he believes you do, he'll keep trying to sow seeds of doubt in you. All you have to do is stay focused, finish the work, and we get back to Bandon."

"Just like that?" I challenged her mildly. "He'll just let me go."

"He may stick around, but we'll be back with a lot more people to watch your back. Remember, he needs you alive. You're the only hope he has of locating Four Twelve."

"So he thinks."

"Exactly," Elaine said, a hint of the ominous in her tone. "Let's hope he doesn't start doubting himself."

Thirty One

Two shots split the deep quiet of the night.

It was near ten o'clock when the warning signal sounded from the east side of the settlement. I was out the door in less than a minute, Elaine remaining with Hope, her MP5 at the ready. As I jogged down Sandy Creek Road and crossed the covered bridge, I saw the Humvee from the outpost pull across the highway and onto the rough gravel road that twisted into a lopsided figure eight. Hart slowed the vehicle to a crawl, allowing me to climb in before continuing on, Corporal Enderson riding shotgun.

"Any idea what this is about?" Enderson asked.

"None," I answered.

We reached the northernmost edge of the road and continued across the field, lights glowing brightly there amongst the trio of temporary tents that had been erected for families to occupy until their houses were made habitable. Hart pulled right up to them, Mike DeSantis standing in the dark with his and two other families. We exited the vehicle and approached, scanning the area for any threats.

"You fired the warnings?" Enderson asked, and Mike nodded.

"Someone reached into our tent," Mike explained. "Reached right under. My daughter saw it and screamed. I just got a glimpse of her hand before she pulled it away."

"It was a woman?" I asked.

"Yeah."

Enderson looked to me. I'd reported to him the encounter with the red-haired woman near our house, and there was little chance that this was someone else.

"Do you want to be point on this, or do you want us to check it out?" Enderson asked.

He'd explained to Mike and Rebecca at our meeting that the responsibility for protecting Remote was theirs, but that the he and Hart would provide any assistance that was necessary. Now, he was putting the first decision in regards to that to one of the settlement's leaders.

"I'd really like to not leave the family right now," Mike said.

His six year old daughter stood in her nightgown and robe between him and his wife, hugging a stuffed bear. She looked up at me, perplexed more than scared.

"Not a problem," Enderson said. "That's what we're here for."

He and Hart started back toward the Humvee, as did I, but Mike DeSantis stopped me.

"Fletch," Mike said, pulling his little girl close with one hand while holding his Mossberg pump with the other.

"Yes?"

"I got a glimpse when I chased after her for a minute," Mike explained.

"Red hair?"

Mike confirmed that with a quick nod. What Elaine and I had seen had filtered beyond Enderson.

"One other thing," Mike said, looking between me and the corporal. "She had a knife. A big one."

* * *

Enderson, Hart, and I backed the Humvee into the open field and left its headlights on, beams cutting into the woods in the direction where Mike had last seen the woman.

"I don't want to kill someone for reaching into a tent for a can of beans," Enderson said.

"We don't know what she was reaching for," I told him.

He had to allow that fact, particularly in light of the report that she was armed. Not as we were, but a blade could be just as deadly as a firearm when wielded by someone trained in its use. Or by someone pushed to the point of desperation.

"Dead or not, those are dense woods to search," Enderson said.

"So we don't search," I said. "We wait."

"Wait?" Hart asked.

"Yeah."

"And where do we wait?" Enderson pressed.

* * *

Ten minutes later the three of us were positioned just below the crest of a hill to the north of Remote, between the tents and my temporary housing. We'd killed the lights and the engine and left the Humvee in the field, traveling on foot, as quiet as we could, to this position of overwatch.

"You're not sure about this at all," Enderson said, his voice hushed. "Are you?"

"It's a hunch," I said.

But, in reality, it was more than that. It was also an admission about the state of humanity, and the state of one particular individual, that did more than sadden me.

I'd noticed the smell when we'd arrived at the tents, some sort of soup cooking on a portable stove within one of the canvas structures. And the night the woman appeared at our house, we'd just put a pot of chicken stew over the fire in the hearth. In the stale, dead world outside, the scent of food, real food, could carry a good distance, and anyone facing hunger would zero in on that indicator of a possible meal.

Just like an animal would.

In my years hunting the Montana and Wyoming wilderness, I'd become accustomed, just as all hunters of any ability had, to letting game trails inform me of where animals would move. From the place they would bed down at night to a source of water. Or food. The red-haired woman had traveled a rough route from my house to the tents, skirting the open space where we'd left the Humvee. The only avenue to accomplish that without taking a wasteful and strenuous detour was directly below where we had perched ourselves.

"Movement," Hart whispered, gesturing slowly with a gloved finger to a point just west of us.

"I'll be damned," Enderson said, shooting me a sideways glance. "You're a wizard."

I shook my head.

"I just like venison," I corrected him.

The woman walked slowly, from tree to tree, taking cover behind the old, dead growth and scanning the way forward before moving again. In the darkness it was impossible to be sure, but I was almost certain I did see something in her right hand. Something large, with a dull shine reflecting in the moonlight filtered through thin clouds.

Enderson gestured to his right, and Hart nodded. The medic would move to a position behind the woman. The corporal nodded to me and pointed to a point ahead of her. He would move straight down the slope toward her.

"We go slow," Enderson cautioned us.

We signaled our understanding with thumbs up, then we moved out. I focused on my assignment, and on the ground beneath me. The soil was damp and loose, no roots of natural ground cover to keep the slope intact. Much had eroded away from the effects of weather. We'd crossed a dozen fallen trees on the way to our initial position, and now I had to traverse them as I moved to cut off the woman's forward progress.

That plan went out the window with the sound of sliding and tumbling to my right.

A quick glance told me that Enderson was on his feet. But beyond him there was only the sight of Hart rolling down the slope, a dislodged length of rotten log chasing him. An errant step had sent him, and it, careening down the hill, and had alerted the woman to our presence.

She bolted. I began running, leaping over the last few obstructions on the hillside, until I could see her sprinting into the open. I could hear Enderson in pursuit off to my right, and Hart recovering beyond him, all three of us part of the chase now.

But the chase did not last long.

Perhaps she had no energy to continue to flee. Or it might have been that she knew we would, eventually, catch up with her. If she'd had a firearm, even a hideaway gun, some .22 revolver of last resort, the confrontation she was about to force would have ended in a fusillade of gunfire. But it did not.

Our chase ended with the red-haired woman stopping in the middle of the open field and spinning to face us, teeth bared against the harsh white of Enderson's weapon light as it came on. She brought the large knife up in her right hand, waving it in the narrowing space between her and us.

"Put the knife down," Enderson ordered her.

Hart slid around to block her retreat, his own M4 trained on her. I sidestepped a bit away from Enderson and did something which might have been foolish—I lowered my AR and let it hang loose from the sling across my chest.

"It's all right," I said. "We're not going to hurt you."

"Yes you are!" the woman screamed at us. "You're from there!"

I had no idea what she was referring to, or where, and I was not qualified to determine if she was suffering serious mental issues, or just suffering. She was thin, but not starved. The clothes she wore, old military BDU pants, a torn black sweatshirt, and mismatched boots, one black and one brown, did not hang off a skeletal frame. So she had survived, somewhere, but was now desperate. And afraid. Of us.

"I promise you," I said, taking a step toward her, "no harm will come to you. Not from us."

She stepped back, bringing the knife up, terror raging in her eyes. Then, without anything said to elicit the change, a sense of calm seemed to settle over her. Her jaw unclenched and her back straightened. The gaze which had burned at us, and directly at me at that moment, began to swim, as if she were about to faint.

But she was not.

"YAAAAAAAAAAAAAAAAAAAHHHHHHHHHHHH!"

The scream she let out, blaring without warning from an otherwise serene face, preceded by a second her hand bringing the knife up, the other rising to add its grip to it, the business end of its blade pointed downward. Right at her own body.

I lunged forward, gloved hands outstretched, reaching for the woman's arms as she started to drive the knife toward her own midsection.

"Fletch!"

Enderson wasn't warning me of any danger. He was reacting to me throwing myself at danger. At the woman who was trying now to kill herself, the blade in her arms about to plunge through tattered material and into precious flesh when my hands batted her aim off its mark. She spun, and I grabbed at the hands she was now drawing back for another attempt on her life. Or on mine.

It didn't matter, though, as two more pairs of hands joined the fight to subdue her, Enderson and Hart each seizing an arm, the medic twisting the weapon from her grip.

"Noooooooooooooo!"

She cried out in protest, collapsing as the reality that she'd failed set in.

"Blood," Hart said, looking to me.

I looked down and saw splashes of bright crimson illuminated by the light swinging at the end of Enderson's M4, the wet stain on my gloves and left arm. But I felt no pain. None at all. Why that was became apparent a second later.

"She's cut," Enderson said.

We lowered the weeping, spent woman to the ground, sobs jerking her body, a flow of blood spilling from a gash on the back of her left hand.

"The blade caught her," Hart said, retrieving a pressure bandage from his cargo pocket and applying it quickly as Enderson and I kept the woman from thrashing.

"Let's get her to the outpost," Enderson said.

We lifted her up and carried her across the fields to the Humvee, knowing two things—we'd caught an intruder, and, more importantly, we'd saved a life. At least for now.

Thirty Two

There'd been no provision for installing any sort of holding cell in the outpost. There were no interior doors at all, in fact. But, as it turned out, none were needed to keep the woman in any sort of custody.

"I'm sorry," she said, looking up from where she sat in the lobby, cup of coffee steaming in her uninjured hand.

Five of us stood facing her, two fresh arrivals joining those of us who'd captured her—Mike DeSantis and Rebecca Vance. The woman seemed most intrigued by her presence. Or her presence among the otherwise exclusively male group looking over her.

"What's your name?"

Enderson asked the question for at least the tenth time, though the other inquiries had been made as we transported the still weeping woman in from the field.

"Dorothy," she said. "I'm Dorothy."

There was no effort to press for a last name, which, for the moment, was a meaningless bit of information. 'Why' was more important than 'who', in this instance.

"Were you looking for food?" I asked.

She hesitated, then nodded, embarrassed. Hunger was something common to admit in the world since the blight began to take its toll. But Dorothy seemed a more recent victim of those effects.

"Where did you come from?" I asked.

"Out there."

"Were you with other people?"

Her gaze dipped, more than embarrassed now. Our probing was taking her to a place she'd left behind. A life she had no desire to revisit.

"Dorothy," Enderson said. "We need to know."

She looked up again, letting her gaze find Rebecca's. They shared a moment, a look, Dorothy's eyes almost pleading as they teared over.

"She doesn't need to talk about that," Rebecca said, running interference for the woman.

I sensed, as did the other men with me, that Dorothy had been through a hell none of us could comprehend. And, as Rebecca was making clear, we had no right to dredge that from the place the woman had tried to bury it.

"You were afraid of us out there," I said. "You said that we were 'from there'. What did you mean?"

"You're from Bandon," she said. "That town on the coast."

"That's right," I said.

"They said...they said you do things to people there. You kill them. For food."

Glances volleyed between those of us who'd come from that very place. A place that was not at all what the woman had been told.

"Who told you this?" Enderson asked.

She tensed, the question requiring an answer that she was not yet ready to give.

"You're safe here," Mike told her, negating the need for any reply. "I promise you that. We all do."

Still, Dorothy regarded us with overt suspicion and distrust.

"Why did you come here?" I asked. "Was it just to get food because you're on your own?"

"Yes," she said. "For food. Just for food."

There was an abrupt insistence to her agreement that more than hinted at some other agenda being present in her appearance in Remote. Everyone in the room could see and hear that.

"Dorothy, it would help us tremendously if you—"

"I think we're done now," Rebecca said, cutting off Enderson's attempt to probe further. "It's already late."

There was no reason to allow Rebecca to dictate the parameters of the questioning, or any end to it. But Corporal Enderson did not seem eager to cross the line she'd just drawn in the sand. Beyond that, it might be best to pick this up in the morning once Dorothy had some time to eat and rest.

"We can find a place for you to stay, Dorothy," Enderson said.

"Can I talk to you all outside?" Rebecca asked, looking to Dorothy. "Will you wait here while I talk to my friends?"

Dorothy nodded and held the still warm mug of coffee against her chest, its heat soaking through her sweatshirt.

We followed Rebecca outside, standing beneath the old overhang, the recently repaired window in front letting us continue observing the woman within.

"She can stay with me," Rebecca Vance said, making any need to search for a host moot.

"That's a generous offer," I said. "But she needs more than we can give her here."

From the corner of my eye I could see Hart nodding.

"Commander Genesee should have a look at her," the medic said. "Especially that hand."

"She stable now, though, yes?" Enderson asked, and again Hart nodded. "Then her staying with Miss Vance will be—"

"Mrs.," Rebecca corrected, the interruption both jarring and sobering. "Mrs."

I'd known Rebecca Vance since I'd arrived in Bandon. Or known of her. She'd always been a private person, with a very close circle of friends. From my place on the very periphery of that circle, I'd never even sensed a hint that the woman had been married.

"Of course," Enderson said. "Dorothy can stay with you, Rebecca, until we can evacuate her."

"Good," Rebecca said.

She waited not a second more, heading back into the outpost and speaking to Dorothy for a moment, the both of them leaving a moment later, passing us as they walked toward the highway and crossed it, disappearing up Sandy Creek Road.

"She's not telling us something," I said.

"She's not telling us a lot," Enderson countered.

It was Mike DeSantis, though, who synthesized the cold reality of the situation for us.

"Isn't that her right?"

There were reasons to disagree with the man, but none were good. If criminals had the right to remain silent, didn't a scared woman who'd suffered unspeakable abuse have the same? Maybe she had even more of a right to say nothing and to tell us to go to hell if we didn't like it.

And, very clearly, in Rebecca Vance she'd found an ally without even knowing she'd been seeking one.

Thirty Three

Dawn broke, grey and cold, thunder rumbling in the distance at the same time a knock sounded on our door.

"At this hour?" Elaine wondered as I left the kitchen where we'd been finishing an early breakfast.

"Someone wants to get started early," I said.

Nick Withers was supposed to come by and head out with me to finish removing roof panels from the storage building next to the outpost. But I wasn't expecting him for another half hour. As it turned out, eagerness to begin the workday wasn't what motivated the interruption of our meal.

Revelation was.

"Fletch," Rebecca Vance said as I opened the door.

Elaine came into the front room behind me, holding Hope.

"Rebecca," my wife said, surprised.

"I'm sorry to come by so early."

"It's all right," I said. "We were already up. Come on in."

I took Rebecca's AK from her and leaned it next to my AR near the door.

"Do you two need to talk?" Elaine asked, ready to leave.

"Yes," Rebecca confirmed. "But you should probably hear this, too."

We sat, Elaine and I on the couch, facing Rebecca, her chair near the fire I'd started just after rising.

"Mike's wife came by with some breakfast for Dorothy a while ago," Rebecca said. "I asked her if she'd just sit with her for a bit so I could come talk to you."

"About what?" I asked.

"We talked last night after I got her back to my place. We talked half the night. When I left, she was still sleeping. She was exhausted to begin with, but getting things off her chest...it drained her."

"What did she tell you?"

"Up until four months ago she was with a group that she'd been with for over a year," Rebecca explained. "She was born and raised in New Mexico, but most of the people she joined up with were from back east. They originally were heading for Eagle One."

"Bandon," Elaine said.

"By the time she found them, they'd given up on that and were mostly scavenging and raiding."

"Raiding," I said. "You mean killing."

"Doing what they had to do to survive," Rebecca said. "Right or wrong didn't matter."

"Right and wrong always matters," Elaine told our guest.

Rebecca nodded at my wife.

"That's what Dorothy said. It's why she split from them. Or tried to. They did to her what you can imagine, if you want to."

"I don't," I said.

"She finally escaped," Rebecca explained. "If she hadn't, she'd be dead. Like the rest of them."

"What happened?" I asked.

"She saw their bodies by the highway between here and Camas Valley."

"The ambush," I said.

"They were the ones who hit you," Rebecca confirmed.

"Wait," Elaine said, shifting her hold on our daughter as she stirred a bit. "If she left them, how did she know about this?"

Again, Rebecca nodded, Elaine keying in on the most salient point of what she'd shared so far.

"That's why I'm here," Rebecca said, looking very purposely to me now. "She threw in with someone else after leaving them."

"Some*one*?" I asked, emphasizing the singular nature of what she'd just said.

"Yeah," Rebecca answered. "A man. With a cowboy hat and a lever action thirty thirty."

"Olin," Elaine said, no surprise in her voice.

And there shouldn't have been. She'd already convinced me that the man who'd killed Neil had to be near, and was trying to get into my head in an effort to find the sample of BA-412. Now, to find out that Dorothy had connected with Tyler Olin, it added a new layer to her appearance in Remote.

"She wasn't just looking for food," I said.

"Last night she was," Rebecca said. "Before that, when you saw her near your place, she was there because he told her to go there. She was supposed to put a couple rocks on your porch, so you couldn't miss them."

Another sign of his presence. Another attempt to trip me up, borrowing from Elaine's Bureau knowledge and training. And, if he was shifting his efforts this close to my home, to my family, it meant he was beginning to press the issue. He was upping his game, either because he felt confident, or because he was getting desperate. Neither option was in the least bit heartening.

"You saw her before she could put the rocks there," Rebecca said. "And when she returned to where Olin had been hiding out by the two creeks south of here, he was gone."

"He'd been supplying her," I said. "Giving her food."

"Exactly," Rebecca said. "He'd use her to spy on places. On people. To leave messages."

"Messages?" Elaine asked. "Messages for who?"

"She didn't know. And she didn't want to know. He was feeding her, and he wasn't hurting her, so she didn't want to do anything to jeopardize that arrangement. She'd just leave a little container with the message wherever he told her to, and pick it up when he told her to."

"She never looked at the messages," I said.

"Like I said, he was keeping her alive. She didn't want to risk that. Plus he was feeding her false information about Bandon."

"Those lies came from him?" I asked.

"Not entirely," Rebecca said, hedging her certainty. "He did push them, but she'd heard them before from the group she was with."

I looked to Elaine.

"You think he was spreading the same rumors to the hiders he encountered?" Elaine wondered. "To poison any perceptions of Bandon?"

"That would explain why we'd had no response to the beacon," I said.

Beckoning people to come to town over the airwaves had resulted in a net population gain of zero. The reason for that might just have been revealed.

"So he tells her all this, uses her, and then he abandons her," Elaine said. "Why?"

"Because she failed," I said. "And he knew she failed. Because he was watching."

I thought for a moment, Rebecca letting me process what she'd shared as the silence lingered. When I'd absorbed all the morsels of information, letting them mentally spin off into likelihoods and possibilities, I looked to the woman who'd brought the news into my home.

"Have you told anyone else?"

Rebecca shook her head.

"Not even Nancy DeSantis?" I pressed.

"No one," Rebecca said, a sense of promise in her words.

"Can we keep it that way?" I asked.

Now she puzzled at me, some true confusion about her.

"Fletch, our radios can relay off the Camas Valley repeater," she said. "You could put out a call and have fifty people here in two hours."

"And he'd just go to ground," I said. "We'd never get him."

"Is that what this is about?" Rebecca asked. "Revenge? Getting him for what he did to Neil Moore?"

To be honest, I wasn't sure if that was my motivation. Or what mainly drove me toward what I'd asked her. But it was part of it. A big part.

"He's dangerous," I reminded our visitor.

"So bring a hundred," Rebecca said. "Get the people from Camas Valley involved. They're your allies now, right? Put that many people in the field and someone will..."

She didn't finish her suggestion. Realization made doing so unnecessary.

"You don't want that," Rebecca said, seeming wary of what she'd just come to understand. "You want to do it yourself."

Elaine seemed ready to counter the assertion. To say that her husband, a new father, was far too realistic to seek out some *mano a mano* resolution with the murderous covert operative. But she didn't. And I knew why. It was my hesitation to do that for myself. To state my own objection to the scenario Rebecca had implied.

"Eric..."

I looked to my wife. There was no way to lie to her. Even if I'd tried, she would have seen right through me.

"He can't get away," I said. "If we bring in the cavalry, we might never see him again."

"And that's a bad thing because..."

My wife's wondering needed no answer. Tyler Olin disappearing would be a victory. But it would not mean the man was defeated. Driving an enemy away was one thing. We'd done that to the Unified Government forces, but they'd simply repositioned and forced the survivors of San Diego into the sea. A sea which swallowed them as their ship likely foundered in the storm near Bandon. If we'd annihilated them, the story would have ended differently for those innocents who'd perished seeking freedom.

Annihilating a force that size, though, was impossible with our resources. Tyler Olin, if he could be located, was one man. And one man could be taken out by another man. An army was not needed.

"Will you keep this quiet, Rebecca?" I pressed her.

She thought for a moment, exchanging a look with Elaine. My wife shook her head and stood, taking our daughter down the hall and closing the door to the bedroom we slept in.

"Will you, Rebecca?"

She needed to consider my request no further.

"You made it so we could come here, Fletch. I suppose someone owes you for doing that."

"Thank you, Rebecca."

She took her AK and left, walking out into the morning mist that hung thick in the fields. I closed the door behind and looked down the hallway, steeling myself before going to the bedroom where Elaine had secluded herself.

When I finally walked in I found her sitting on the end of the bed, cradling Hope, tears skimming her eyes.

"We were going to go back to Bandon," she said.

"We still are."

"Back there we'd have people around us. People to watch your back. I told you this."

"Elaine..."

She shook her head, not wanting to hear any explanation I could offer.

"Are you some avenging angel? Is that how you see yourself?"

"He's not going to stop," I told her. "Until someone stops him."

"You mean until you stop him."

"He's communicating with people," I said. "You heard Rebecca. For all we know he could have coordinated that ambush. It could have been his idea."

"You really believe that?" Elaine challenged me. "How does you ending up dead on the highway get him what he wants?"

She had more than a point. I was reaching, searching for any justification to show that Olin was already too dangerous for us to allow him another chance to get away. But he was in contact with someone, if Dorothy was to be believed. Someone who...

Wait...

"Hold on," I said, my gaze shifting to the window as I thought. "Something's not right."

"Of course something's not right," Elaine said, too loud, our daughter whimpering in her sleep. "You want to put yourself up against a man who kills for a—"

"No, not that," I said.

Elaine calmed, sensing that I was struggling with some internal doubt.

"What is it?"

"Dorothy went all in with Olin for food," I recounted. "Rebecca said that, right?"

"Right."

"So, tell me this—where did he get the food to give her?"

My unsatisfied curiosity now infected Elaine. She puzzled over the same incongruity, likely facing the same obstacle to full understanding which vexed me. He could not have carried enough food to supply both himself and another, even if he'd had some cached somewhere, or if

he'd been resupplied by his masters back at the CIA. He
had to have a local food source, for both himself, and for
any he would bribe with sustenance.

"Camas Valley," I said.

"Dalton?"

"No," I said. "Ansel and Moira. It makes sense."

Elaine was coming to the same conclusion that I had.

"He had them break into our house," she said. "The
first play at tripping you."

"Every other break-in was a diversion," I said. "Just
like Martin thought."

"And if you think you're targeted, that's the paranoia,"
Elaine said. "All part of his plan."

"It might have worked," I said. "If I'd known where
Four Twelve was, I would have checked on it to make sure it
was secure."

Elaine placed our bundled daughter on the bed and
came close to me, her voice low.

"Eric, I was wrong. You need protection here now. We
all do. Put a call into Schiavo. At least have her send a
couple more of her people out here."

I heard my wife's request, not quite to the point of
begging, but not far from it, either. Still, my mind was
elsewhere, chewing on Olin's connection to Ansel and
Moira. There was no direct proof of their communication,
or their collusion, but even the possibility raised more
questions than it answered.

"Elaine," I said, ignoring what she'd just said. "We
know what Olin gets from them. He gets food, and people
to do his dirty work. But what do they get from him?"

"Are you not listening to me?" Elaine pressed me. "This
is too much, okay? He's not just some well-trained spook.
He's more than that. Do you see that?"

I looked to her, still glossing over her concern.

"What do they get for helping him?"

She grabbed my shirt, bunching its front in her fists.

"Are you even hearing me?"

"You're right," I said. "This is bigger. If Dalton's people are involved with him, then we have to tread carefully. Schiavo was afraid to jeopardize the alliance, but I think she undersold the possible consequences."

"What are you talking about?"

"I'm talking about an ally becoming an enemy," I said, then headed for the front door.

Elaine stepped into the hallway, worried. Even more so when she saw me pull my vest and all its associated gear from the closet.

"Eric, what are you doing?"

"If you truly care for me, you'll keep this between us," I said. "I need you to trust me. Please."

For a moment, she just stood there, silent, not ignoring my plea. Rather, it seemed she knew how she wanted to respond, but couldn't, because it would crush me. In the end, she simply stepped back into the bedroom with our daughter and closed the door.

I could have gone to her. I should have gone to her. But I didn't. If I had, I might have given in to her and done what conventional thinking pointed to being the smart course of action.

None of this, though, was conventional. It was anything but. A man who'd honed his skills deceiving and killing for a living had interjected himself into our lives. He'd killed, and, if I was correct, he was going to kill again, by proxy, and in larger numbers. All to force me to give him something I could not. And if I were to tell him that, to come clean as to my ignorance about the location of BA-412, would he even believe me?

No. He would not.

If he was coopting Ansel and Moira, I had to have absolute proof of that. Something tangible that I could take to Schiavo. Only then would she feel justified in bringing the treachery to Dalton's attention before it could manifest itself in ways both dangerous and deadly for the people of Remote, and the residents of Bandon.

I could expect Elaine to understand why I had to do what I was doing, but I knew she would not accept it. And there was no point in trying. She believed I was guided by the desire for vengeance. I was. But there was a larger component to my reason now. If Olin were to turn on me, I might end up dead. If Camas Valley turned against us, the bodies would end up being stacked like cordwood.

Thirty Four

'*By the two creeks.*'

That was the extent of the directions to Olin's former hideout I had, shared second hand by Rebecca. I knew the area. The exact spot, actually. On a patrol some time ago, before there was ever an idea of Remote as a settlement, we'd scouted the confluence of the creeks, which then flowed north into the Coquille River. Some suggestion that a distant hydro power station could be built there had taken place, with the long term plan of providing electricity for road maintenance crews who would have to overnight while performing repairs on bridges and roads. That plan hadn't yet been moved from concept to action, but the location was prime. For many things.

Boulders had been naturally piled where the two creeks joined, placed by erosion and landslides that shaped the terrain over thousands of years. The massive slabs of rock reminded me of where Olin had holed up near Bandon, in the space between two giant knobs of granite. It didn't surprise me that the man had, apparently, chosen a similar landscape to hide amongst in this area.

The creeks were brimming, high on runoff from the recent snows, and topped off by rain which fell almost daily in varying amounts. I crossed the first creek atop a fallen tree which was too thick to have rotted to the point of failing. The second stretch of racing water I leapt, jumping from a high point on one bank to a wide, low spot on the opposite side, slick ground causing me to momentarily lose my footing, sending me forward into a bulbous boulder. The impact knocked the wind out of me and I dropped to my knees, trying to gulp air quietly. I did not expect that Olin would be in or near a hideout he had apparently abandoned, but I also knew that his interest was in me.

I'd taken what precautions I could when setting out to locate where he'd hidden. After informing Nick that he'd be working alone for the day, I had him drop me two miles west on the side of the highway. From there I'd crossed to the south and angled my way toward the twin creeks, where I now knelt, gasping for air.

After a minute I'd regained enough composure to continue, weaving my way through the maze of boulders which lay next to and atop each other, creating a multi-level maze with dozens of hiding spaces. I searched every single one I could find, scouring the ground within and nearby, hoping to find a can, a wrapper, anything that would tie this spot to some supply from Camas Valley.

But there was nothing. Not a scrap of paper. Not a boot print in the muck. There was no evidence that would be useful in tying Olin to supplies from Camas Valley, and to Ansel and Moira.

Unless you're wrong...

That errant bit of self-doubt surfaced as I continued through the warren of jumbled boulders. Except, I wasn't wrong. Ansel and Moira were trusted aides to Dalton. This was obvious after seeing their interaction at our first meeting. Others we'd crossed paths with, Lo and Gina, for example, were, for lack of a better term, foot soldiers. They had not been in the inner sanctum as Dalton met with us.

Even if I was right, though, simply believing so was not justification enough to bring the matter to Schiavo, who might, just *might*, take it to Dalton. *If* there was true proof that Olin had been in contact with the man's top people.

But that evidence proved entirely elusive as I searched the last hollows and overhangs created by the ancient fall of boulders. My journey here, in addition to putting a very real strain on my relationship with Elaine, had been pointless. There was no discovery to be made.

As I retraced my steps through the tangle of massive rocks, I did not berate myself for failing. I did, however, revisit one very certain thing concerning Olin—he was damn good at his craft. He'd kept me, and the leadership of Bandon, in the dark as to his true motives, while carefully readying himself to take out his colleague and my friend. He was ruthless and cunning, careful to a fault, physically fit and mentally sharp. He was a hard man with a disarming smile and a probing stare. He marked his enemies while they still saw him as friendly at best, and harmless at worst.

And all those things, that full package that was Tyler Olin, was as gone from his apparent hideout as he could be. The area had been sanitized. Not even a boot print remained.

I came around the final array of boulders, back to the space where I had landed when jumping across the second creek and stumbling. I would have to find a different way to the far bank, I knew, though doing so became suddenly unimportant as I saw what lay on the slippery ground.

Two small stones, arranged next to each other. Identical to what I'd seen in the storage building. And in Olin's original hideout.

The man was here. Close.

"Olin!"

I called out to him, charging forward and bounding into the creek, high stepping through the waist-high water and scrambling up the opposite, muddy shore. My boots finally found purchase on the soggy earth and I ran through the trees, scanning left and right, my AR sweeping fast one direction, then the other. I'd been in the maze of boulders for fifteen minutes, plenty of time for the man to leave his calling card and fade away into the woods.

But he wouldn't do that. He would want to see the result of his handiwork. Want to see my reaction.

"OLIN!"

I screamed his name as loud as I could, the volume half natural, and half manufactured. If the man wanted me to teeter toward some unhinged break, I was going to let him be witness to just that. Truthfully, though, I was enraged, at his presence, and at his ability to move ghost-like in and out of my life. Had Elaine not recognized his methods, the reaction I was partially feigning right now might have been coming from a more desperate place.

No response came from the dead woods. But he was out there. That I was certain of. I backed through the grey stands of trees, toward the creek I'd just forded. Once there I followed it north until I reached the first creek, using a series of wide stones to easily walk across it. With only the forest between me and the highway now, I stopped and looked back, expecting to see nothing. And no one. Olin might not be watching me anymore. Seeing me come upon what he'd left for me back at the boulders had likely been satisfying enough for him.

Still I stared out into the once lush landscape. We were trying to bring life to the land again. He was seeking that which could render the planet devoid of life for good. His reasons for wanting BA-412 mattered not at all to me. It was best that Neil had not entrusted its location to me. That meant Olin could use every trick he had, and I could still not lead him to it. And if I did know where it was...

I'd die trying to keep him from it.

Part Four

Showdown

Thirty Five

As I stood with Enderson at the counter in the garrison's outpost, going over plans for minor street repairs in Remote, a sound, both familiar and strange, rose in the near distance.

The corporal and I stepped outside of the repurposed general store and looked east, in the direction of the odd whining, a low rooster tail of dust spinning above a collection of vehicles coming our way. Motorcycles.

In Cheyenne, when Neil, Elaine, and I had been captured by Moto and his band of cannibal thugs, I'd been dragged to town behind a makeshift electric cycle powered by a beefy collection of car batteries. What approached us was nowhere near as crude.

Dalton was in the lead, two more bikes just behind, Gina and Moira riding the nearly silent two wheelers as the trio neared us and stopped, no final throaty cough of an internal combustion engine to signal that the motor had been turned off. Their mastery of battery technology and production, not to mention coupling those power sources to small and powerful motors, was impressive.

"Good morning," Dalton said, dropping his bike's kickstand and stepping off.

He wore goggles but no helmet, and slipped that eyewear off. Behind him, the two women dismounted their rides, hanging back, Gina's Remington shotty slung across her back and Moira's AK ready in front at the end of a single point sling. Dalton carried no long weapon. But in the front of his waistband, violating every rule of gun safety, a stainless steel revolver was tucked inside his belt. A .357 I thought after a quick glance. Big enough to take a foot, and anything north of that, off with one unintentional pull of the trigger.

"Good morning," Enderson said, stepping forward and offering his hand. "We haven't met. I'm Corporal—"

"Mo Enderson," Dalton said. "Not Morris."

Enderson smiled.

"And you must be Dalton," he said.

"You'll find introductions aren't really necessary," I told the corporal. "We're a known quantity."

Dalton gave me a look. Not angry, not appreciative. It was simply a cold, silent acknowledgment that I was there.

"We received the supplies," Dalton said.

A week we'd been in Remote. The day before, a convoy of trucks, the same ones which had brought us to the new settlement, had rumbled past, heading east to Camas Valley. Martin was in the lead vehicle and offered a wave as the four trucks passed. A few hours later, on their return trip, the convoy stopped briefly to check on us and report on their contact with the Camas Valley community. All had gone as expected in the exchange, one of the trucks now carrying boxes of batteries for delivery to Bandon. This visit by Dalton and his rather small entourage was, I suspected, to confirm that their end of the agreement which formalized our alliance was being fulfilled.

"And we've scouted the areas north and south of you," the man added.

Enderson nodded at the report.

"Anything we need to know?" I asked.

"Minor movement," Dalton said. "A few hiders out and about. Nothing to be concerned with."

"Didn't some of these hiders ambush our people between here and Camas Valley?" Enderson asked, without expecting any reply. "I'd be concerned with those kind of people."

"Those kind of people are all dead," Dalton said, shifting his attention briefly to me. "Aren't they?"

His people had saved Schiavo, Hart, and me from being overrun in an isolated spot, and had taken out every last attacker. People who Dorothy had fled from months before. Rebecca had kept her word and hadn't shared anything which she'd told me. Nor had Elaine, though my asking her to remain silent about the revelations gleaned from Dorothy had brought a chill to our relationship.

"Dead and gone," I concurred.

"We're sweeping east and west of you right now," Dalton continued. "But the hiders avoid the highway."

"Except when they're trying to kill you," I interjected.

The man shook his head at that suggestion.

"They don't try to kill us," Dalton corrected. "They try to kill you."

Enderson sensed the uncomfortable shift in the exchange. I was challenging the leader of Camas Valley, for no reason other than some attempt to get under his skin. But that tactic wasn't without some purpose in mind.

"Right," I said. "So, will any hiders out there who might be hostile see this settlement as an extension of you, or of Bandon?"

Dalton thought for a moment, realizing where I was going with my probing.

"You're asking if Remote will enjoy safety by association," the man said, pondering the possibility for a moment. "Mostly."

"So there will still be threats out there," Enderson said.

"There are always threats," Dalton confirmed. "Everyone has a bullet with their name on it. Only question is whether you're downrange when it's fired."

He looked back to Gina and nodded. She unstrapped a box from the back of her motorcycle and brought it forward, holding it out. Enderson took the package, its weight settling his grip downward until he compensated.

"Some batteries for your outpost," Dalton said, and Gina retreated to her motorcycle.

"Thank you," Enderson said. "We had someone come into the town the other night. A woman."

Dalton accepted the report with a nod.

"Women alone don't last long out there," he said, tipping his head toward the dead woods.

"We didn't get much out of her," Enderson said, truthfully ignorant of what the woman had shared with Rebecca. "She could have been hooked up with a group of hiders."

"I'd think that was a definite," Dalton agreed. "What are you doing with her?"

"We sent her back to Bandon with the convoy," Enderson explained.

That didn't surprise Dalton, but it didn't seem acceptable, either.

"We need to work out some arrangement where any arrivals can choose where to settle," Dalton suggested, though the hint of determination in his words made the idea seem more than simply something which might come to pass. "Here, with us, or in Bandon."

Enderson didn't disagree with the proposal, but didn't accept it, either. He couldn't. And he knew that Dalton knew that.

"That sound like a reasonable proposal to be discussed," the corporal said. "I'll let Remote's leaders and Bandon's know your thoughts on the issue."

Dalton was smart enough to not push the matter. But he was also savvy enough to realize that whatever insistence he hinted at would carry its own weight in any decision. Regardless, at the end of the day, anyone who found their way to any of our communities was free to choose where their long term home would be. Even in Camas Valley, where it might appear that Dalton ruled with an amply padded iron fist, someone wanting to leave would not be forced to stay, I knew. Unwilling and unhappy inhabitants of any group were an annoyance at best, and a liability at worst.

"Good," Dalton said, reaching to the goggles he'd shifted to the top of his head.

"Quick question," I said.

The man left his eye protection where it was and looked to me.

"What's your range on those things?"

Dalton glanced to his motorcycle, smiling.

"You mean, could my people use these to quietly approach Bandon and scout it from the outskirts for months without being detected?"

He'd read the intent of where my probing was going.

"The answer is yes," he said, then lowered his goggles and remounted his bike.

"The settlement's leaders have asked about meeting you," Enderson told the man. "Everybody over there would like to, I believe."

Over there was just across the highway, in Remote proper. It was apropos, I had thought, that the representatives of the place they had separated from existed, at least temporarily, on the opposite side of a road. The man-made delineation point between the garrison's outpost and the settlers had, oddly, served to keep relations cordial so far, it seemed to me. Had Enderson and Hart been billeted in a house amongst those whose suspicions toward government ran high, the lingering distrust could have festered. Or boiled over.

"We'll oblige," Dalton said.

He steered his cycle past us, Gina and Moira following, the pitch of the electric motors whining high as they cruised back to the highway and crossed over to meet their new neighbors.

"Did I pick up some vibe between you two?" Enderson asked when we were alone. "Because my orders are to keep Remote safe and to service the alliance. If you have some issue with him..."

"No issue," I said. "No issue at all."

He took my assurance at face value and turned back toward the outpost.

"Mo..."

Enderson looked back to me.

"Dalton knows more about us than we do about him," I said. "Remember that when you're servicing the alliance."

It wasn't a slap at the corporal, and he didn't take it that way. He did, however, seem to mull what I'd just reminded him of, before giving me a quick nod and returning to the outpost.

Thirty Six

We continued to work, repairing and refitting houses, and streets, and plumbing, and power systems. In less than two weeks, most of Remote was almost ready to be branded a livable town.

Not everything, though, had been fixed. Nor could it be in so short a time.

Elaine and I had come to a point of existing with one another. We spoke, we ate, we cared for and played with our daughter. But something was missing. Something had evaporated from the life we'd known together. We still loved each other, but my insistence on dealing with Olin in ways as covert as his very nature had changed our dynamic. The spontaneous joy that had developed between us over time was now virtually non-existent.

For days there had been no sign of Olin, or his presence. No markers that would indicate any further attempt to play with my mind had been found. In a way, the absence of any hint of him being close was disquieting. One might think he had abandoned his efforts and departed, slipping away again, for good, or just relocating as he bided his time.

I knew better. So did Elaine. When night came and we readied ourselves for bed, the Glock she had been leaving in its holster atop her gear bag now rested on an upturned crate that served as a nightstand next to the bed. My Springfield was similarly close, and my AR, left by the front door since arriving in our temporary home, lay on the floor next to my boots. Neither of us were afraid, but we both knew that Olin would not wait forever.

We slept. In fits and starts. She stared at the curtained window. I tuned my ear to all sounds, both inside and outside our house. She saw nothing. I heard nothing.

But something would come. Olin would not stop. And he would not wait forever. A clock we could not see was already ticking down toward some act we could not anticipate.

"Eric."

We faced away from each other in bed, back to back, some slight separation between our bodies.

"Yes?"

I felt her hand reach behind and settle upon my hip, palm up, fingers splayed, waiting for me. My hand slipped across my chest and took hold of hers. She squeezed tight, as if wanting to know, and wanting me to know, that we were still *us*.

"I love you," she said.

I nodded against my pillow.

"I love you, too."

"We're going to be okay," she told me. "We are."

"I know," I said.

What had wounded us as a couple had not been erased, nor forgotten. I didn't know if it ever would be. And maybe it should not be. Some cuts, the deepest ones, scarred over, making that place of pain tougher than what surrounded it. Marriage could be that way, I supposed, my far from expert opinion willing to accept that possibility.

"We'll work this out," I promised her.

Her grip on my hand bore down again, a thankful pressure. I rolled to face her, and she to face me. In the moonlight filtering through the curtained window I could see tears streaming silently down her cheeks. I reached up and wiped them away with the back of my hand.

"Get some sleep," I told her.

My hand caressed her face, and her eyes closed. We lay there, facing each other now. Her breathing became slow and calm as she drifted off. I remained awake, watching her, my gaze shifting every so often to the window beyond, looking for shadows that should not be there. None appeared. We were safe.

That would all change in less than twelve hours.

Thirty Seven

Just before noon someone knocked on our door.

Elaine held Hope close in our living room and stepped to the side so she could see past the sheer curtains we'd put up over the front windows of our temporary home.

"It's a woman," my wife said. "I don't recognize her."

I'd shed my sidearm, coming home for a quick bite before returning to work on one of the settlement's final projects, but my AR, which had been in the bedroom as we slept, now leaned against the wall just beyond where the door would swing when opened. In two seconds I could have it in hand.

"She's got a shotgun," Elaine added.

There were a few people it could be, but only one I thought it might be.

"A Remington semi?"

Elaine nodded. I left my AR where it was and opened the front door. Gina from Camas Valley stood in the shallow shelter of the small porch, rain that she'd just come through dripping from her coat.

"I have to talk to you."

Those were her words. But they seemed more like the declaration of some personal mission. She'd come on her own, on a motorcycle across the hills that separated Remote from Camas Valley, leaving her transport in the woods just north of our town. After a brief description of her travels I invited her in and took her drenched outerwear, hanging it on a hook behind the door.

"Can you take this?" she asked, holding her shotgun out to me.

I did, leaning the weapon next to mine. It seemed that she carried no other firearms. None that I could see, in any case. In all likelihood she had at least one pistol on her person. That near certainty, though, didn't concern me. Nothing about her unannounced appearance, nor her demeanor, hinted at any threat. At least not from her.

"Sit," I said. "We have some hot chocolate."

The offer amazed her slightly as she took a spot on the couch.

"Hot chocolate?"

I nodded. The cream of their supplies had run out some time ago, it seemed. Ours, too, was beginning to run low with the *Rushmore* being absent from the waters off Bandon.

"Made with water, not milk," Elaine said.

I caught myself, having failed at both host and husband duties.

"This is my wife—"

"Elaine," Gina said. "I know."

It was easy to forget how completely the people of Camas Valley had come to know us through their observation, and though it seemed somewhat creepy at first, it now entered exchanges such as this with almost comical regularity.

"But I don't know this little beauty," Gina said, her gaze fixed on our daughter.

"This is Hope," Elaine said.

Gina smiled. Beamed, actually, the brightness of her reaction to the infant before her bringing a warmth to the room that had nothing to do with heat.

"Would you like to hold her?" Elaine asked, surprising the woman.

"I'm soaked," she said. "I'm already dripping on your furniture."

"She's wrapped up," Elaine said. "It'll be okay."

Gina thought on the offer for a moment, both surprised and pleased by the hospitality, and the trust, we were showing her.

"Okay."

"I'll get that hot chocolate," I said.

I retrieved a cup of the steaming liquid, returning to the front room to find Elaine sitting next to Gina, the woman cradling our daughter as one would something precious beyond measure.

"Do you have children?" Elaine asked, taking Hope back so Gina could accept the hot mug from me.

"No. Someday. Maybe."

She sipped the chocolatey drink, then drank steadily, savoring what she had not enjoyed for a very long time. But she had not come on a social visit, though we had done our best to make her feel welcome.

"You wanted to talk to me," I said, nudging the conversation forward.

Gina nodded and set her cup on the side table.

"Dalton and Lo headed north this morning to scout Winston," she told me.

"And?"

"That leaves Ansel in charge," she said, seeming to hesitate.

"You mean Ansel and Moira," I said.

The woman's relief was plain that I was picking up on the reality of a situation she had to live with.

"They're bad news together," Gina said. "But..."

Her reluctance to speak now was more visceral, some fear, either real or perceived, clearly manifesting. I had a reasonable idea precisely what it was driving her concern. Or, more accurately, who.

"It's Dalton," I said. "Isn't it?"

Gina looked between me and Elaine.

"Whatever you say here isn't leaving these walls," Elaine assured her.

"He's kept us alive," Gina said, an almost awestruck appreciation in her words. "That's impossible to minimize."

Just as Martin had guided Bandon through the worst of the blight, Dalton, in Camas Valley, had seen to the survival of his people, though with a more authoritarian edge. Gina, though, wasn't devaluing his accomplishment because of that, or in any way. She simply was having trouble relating that the man to whom she owed her life was flawed.

"He doesn't see it," Gina said. "Ansel is just...he's wrong. I've heard him talking to Moira about how they could run things better. How they could force you all to..."

"To what?" I asked.

"To give them tribute," she said. "After Dalton made the agreement with you, Ansel told Moira that he could have gotten more just by threatening to destroy your fields and your livestock. He said paying us off with supplies would be cheaper for Bandon."

I looked to Elaine. We were both thinking the same thing. Regardless of what Schiavo wanted, or how removed she wanted to remain from the inner workings of Camas Valley, Dalton had to be made aware of this.

"You think Ansel and Moira are going to make a move to topple Dalton while he's gone today?"

She didn't signal agreement or otherwise to the question I posed. But her gaze darkened. Grim worry washed over her.

"They went somewhere," Gina said. "After Dalton left, they did, too. On foot. I followed them."

"Where did they go?" I asked.

"They went out to this old clear cut grove about two miles south of the highway. Just piles and piles of old dead trees there. The loggers must have been in the middle of harvesting timber when everything went to hell. I mean, why keep working when the world is ending, right?"

"What did they do there?" I asked.

"I didn't get very close," Gina explained. "If they'd seen me..."

"You'd be dead," Elaine suggested.

Gina didn't dispute that one iota.

"They met with someone," Gina said.

Neither Elaine nor I had any doubt who she was going to describe.

"Cowboy hat with a scoped lever action?" I asked.

Gina nodded through surprise.

"How did you..."

"We've had dealings with him," Elaine said, looking to me. "You were right—this is bigger."

She'd remembered what I'd told her in the heat of our disagreement. And she'd kept an open mind about it as I'd trudged off in search of evidence. Evidence which we now had in Gina's eyewitness account.

"Gina," I began, "will you tell Dalton this, if I'm with you to back you up?"

The woman hesitated, running through the ramifications of turning on two of their leader's lieutenants. We'd assured her that she could speak freely with us, and it would go no further. But it needed to, and if it did, it had to happen with her participation.

"Do you know what you're asking me to do?"

"I do," I told her. "You'll be putting your life on the line."

"So will you," Gina reminded us.

I glanced to Elaine, and she nodded, willing to accept the risk I would face.

"Dalton has to be told," I said.

"I know," Gina agreed, both resignation and determination in her voice as she spoke again. "I know."

"Any idea when Dalton will be back?" I asked.

She shook her head.

"He'd only share that information with Ansel," she said.

"You could try to cut him off before he gets back from Winston," Elaine suggested. "Wait for him on the road north of Camas Valley."

I thought on that, and could see that Gina was considering the feasibility of such an attempt.

"The bike has the range," she said.

"Going over land?" I asked. "With a rider and passenger?"

"Yeah," she confirmed. "Just enough."

I looked to Elaine again. None of what was about to come was ideal, but we both knew that, if warning Dalton prevented a takeover of his town, it would solidify the nascent alliance between Camas Valley and Bandon. And, if Olin's connection with Ansel and Moira was as Gina had described, Dalton would have every reason to turn his forces against the man who'd murdered my friend and was stalking me.

"This is the best of a lot of bad options," Elaine said.

I nodded and looked to the woman who'd risked her life to bring us the information we now had to act upon.

"Can you bring your bike around back?"

"All right."

I walked her to the door, Elaine with me as I handed Gina her shotty. She stepped onto the porch and hesitated, turning to face me again.

"Dalton was right," she said.

"About what?" I asked.

"You. He said you have grit. I've only heard him say that about one other person."

"Who was that," Elaine asked.

"His father."

I was both humbled and buoyed by the praise she was sharing. The few times I'd challenged Dalton, however mildly, had apparently made some impression upon him.

"I'll get a light load of gear," I said, knowing every ounce of weight would burden the electric bike and shorten its range.

"As light as possible," Gina said. "If we—"

That was her last word—we. At the instant it slipped past her lips a gush of tissue and blood erupted from where her face had been, the crack of a rifle sounding next as her dead body folded, landing with a thud on the porch.

"Get down!"

I shouted the warning to Elaine as I slammed the door shut and scrambled on all fours across the room, away from my AR, rushing to get my Springfield from the belt rig hanging off the back of a chair. Behind me, Elaine had grabbed her MP5 from just outside the closet and was sliding to cover in the hallway, Hope awake and crying.

"Stay low!"

There was no need to instruct my wife in how to stay safe, but instinct made me call out as I reached up from my position on the floor and grabbed a lamp. I heaved the fixture hard at a window I'd repaired the first day we'd arrived, shattering the old glass, creating an opening that I stuck my pistol through and pulled the trigger twice, aiming into the air outside.

* * *

Enderson and Hart were there within three minutes, and a dozen others from the settlement were geared up and patrolling the town's border.

"He had to be close," Enderson said, looking down at the body lying in a bloody pool, old boards soaking in the crimson flow as rain pattered on the roof above. "In this weather, his sightline would be a hundred yards, tops."

His...

I'd told the corporal it was Olin. Without a doubt. The same crack of his rifle had sounded when Neil was shot down, that distinctive .30-30 impossible to miss.

"He's still out there," I said.

"Eric..."

I looked past the body to my wife just inside as Hart carried a small tarp from the Humvee and covered Gina. Gina whose last name was a mystery to us, but whose actions had given us some warning as to what was happening in Camas Valley. Or what might have already happened.

"Tell him," Elaine said.

I knew what she meant. There was no point in withholding anything from Enderson anymore. Moves were being made that could jeopardize the lives of everyone in Remote.

"Olin's been here," I said. "For a while."

Enderson and Hart listened as I explained everything. What I'd found, what I'd seen, and what we'd been told.

"Jesus, Fletch," Enderson said. "What do you think I would have done if you'd shared this when it all happened?"

"Go after him," I said. "And send him into hiding."

Enderson shook his head, annoyed at my actions.

"Mo, be pissed at me all you want, but we have to act. Right now."

I didn't have to spell anything out for the corporal. He knew what had to be done, and as Mike DeSantis jogged up to report that the patrols had found nothing so far, Enderson took the first steps needed to bring some order to a chaotic situation.

"Mike," Enderson said.

"Yeah?"

"Get Rebecca and Nick and meet us at the outpost. We have to talk."

Thirty Eight

"No."

Rebecca Vance's response to what Enderson had just told Remote's leadership was as simple as it could be.

"We're not leaving," she added, just to make clear her insistence.

"It's not permanent," I said. "But there's a real threat. Camas Valley could have just been taken over in a coup."

"What?!" Mike DeSantis exclaimed, shaking his head. "How can you possibly know that?"

"We don't," I said. "But it's a certainty that a power struggle is underway, and if it goes wrong, Remote will have a hostile population just to the east."

"There won't be time for help to arrive from Bandon if things turn sour," Enderson added.

Mike looked to Nick Withers, then to Rebecca. The leaders of the Remote settlement wore mixed reactions— resistance, disbelief, fear. Already the settlers had gathered at three houses along Sandy Creek Road, mine included, to maintain a localized defense against possible threats that were seeming more probable by the minute.

"You want to evacuate everyone?" Nick asked, checking that he was following what was being proposed. "Everyone?"

"With the cars, pickups, the Humvee, and the supply truck, we can fit everyone," Enderson assured them.

The big military truck, which had brought a load of supplies to Remote late the previous day, had overnighted to allow its driver and security rider time to rest. It could be packed with twenty people for the relatively short drive back to Bandon.

"Why not just radio for reinforcements to come here?" Mike asked.

"Because we're cut off," I said.

"The repeater in Camas Valley isn't responding," Enderson said. "We have no radio link with anyone in Bandon."

That bit of sobering information sank in for a moment before anyone responded. When they did, it was Rebecca, though her thinking was still far from cooperative and accepting.

"And if we say no?"

"Rebecca..."

Mike DeSantis tried to nudge her gently, his tone concerned. But she was having none of it.

"And if we say no?" she repeated.

"Rebecca," Enderson began, "it appears to me that you may be the only person taking that position."

She looked to her fellow leaders and found no ally to support her resistance. Accepting what was being proposed, or ordered, depending on one's viewpoint, was almost beyond what she could accept. Almost.

"If we'd just done this on our own without this alliance garbage," she said, suggesting an alternate path the settlers might have taken.

"You'd still be facing what could be coming down that highway at any minute," I told her. "Without any real way to resist."

"Running is resisting?" she challenged me.

"Here, yes," I said.

I'd run before. From Missoula to my refuge north of Whitefish when the blight struck. To Eagle One when my refuge became an untenable position to maintain. I'd never returned to either place I'd occupied, but here, there was that chance for Rebecca Vance, and for all who'd decided to make Remote their home.

"This is the smart move, Rebecca," Enderson said.

She drew a breath and looked to the misty daylight beyond the outpost's front windows. Some thought seemed to seize her. Or some dark memory.

"My husband and I turned tail and ran," she said, still focused on the lessening weather outside. "We ran from our home when gangs were raiding neighborhoods around us for food. There were no police, no soldiers. There was only us."

She stopped there, the recollection taking hold of her fully now.

"The gangs shot him when he tried to drive through a barricade they set up," she explained, eyes welling. "He was dead and I was flooring it and steering from the passenger seat to get away as they kept shooting."

Mike DeSantis reached out and put a hand on her shoulder. She reached up and rested her hand atop his, accepting the gesture of comfort.

"Running from thugs is not something that's easy for me to accept," she said.

"We'll be back," Nick told her, trying to soothe her with words of promise.

She nodded, then looked to Enderson and me and nodded again.

"Okay," she said.

Enderson wasted no time, because no one knew how long we had before a move by those who may have taken over Camas Valley.

"Let's have everyone meet on the highway in fifteen minutes," the corporal directed. "Personal weapons, medications, and that's it. We're going to be tight on room. Have your drivers bring their vehicles. Clear?"

It was.

Something, though, was still unclear to me as the meeting broke up—Olin's part in this. Was he advising Ansel and Moira, or was he providing more direct assistance? Whichever it was, it was certain that he had some move in mind that he was going to make. And, considering the proximity to my family of what he'd unleashed less than an hour ago, I had no confidence that he was sticking to any plan he'd been executing to this point. The game had changed, and he knew that. Gina's presence in Remote was obviously something to which he had reacted violently.

We were running, I knew, but he wouldn't.

Thirty Nine

The vehicles were loaded and ready to roll twenty minutes after the meeting had finished, the convoy rumbling on the highway, pointed west.

"What's Schiavo going to do?" Elaine asked, sitting in the passenger seat of our pickup, Hope in one arm, MP5 in her free hand.

"I don't know," I said. "I suppose it depends on how bad things turn in Camas Valley."

The truth be told, I wasn't even thinking on such a macro level at the moment. My thoughts were consumed by Tyler Olin and trying to imagine, guess, anticipate what the man was going to do next. How close were his ties with Ansel and Moira? Much of what he might attempt depended upon that. If he held more sway than just bartering for food with them, he might have a willing fighting force in any post-coup makeup of Camas Valley.

No...

His motives were not that grand. He wanted what I knew he wanted—BA-412. His focus was that. Whatever he had arranged with Ansel and Moira had to service that need. A need that still existed.

"Enderson's coming," Elaine said.

My driver's window was already down. The corporal, in full gear, jogged up, his M4 at the ready.

"I'm three vehicles up in the Humvee," Enderson said. "Will you bring up the rear? I'm putting Nick in your truck bed to cover our tail."

Nick Withers hurried past the sedan just ahead of us and gave a wave as he climbed into the empty cargo area of our pickup and took a knee, his AK already pointed at the empty highway behind us.

"Sure thing," I said.

"Okay," Enderson said. "Let's roll out."

The corporal moved quickly past the vehicles ahead. Engines revved. Diesel smoke belched into the air from the supply truck as the convoy began to move.

All but our pickup.

"Eric..."

I looked to Elaine and took my AR from where it lay on the seat between us, opening the driver's door and stepping out.

"Slide over and take the wheel," I told my wife.

"What are you doing?" she asked, confused and concerned.

"Fletch, what's going on?"

"Nick, just cover the rear. Elaine is driving."

"I'm what? I have Hope."

I reached in and took my wife by the arm, pulling her across the bench seat until she was positioned to drive, the MP5 now on the seat where she'd been sitting.

"You're going twenty miles an hour," I said. "You can do this. You *have* to."

"What are you doing?" she pressed me.

I gave her and our daughter quick kisses, then closed the door.

"If I go to Bandon, he's going to follow," I said. "This has to end."

"Eric..."

"The convoy is getting ahead of us," Nick said, his own worry showing.

"Go," I told Elaine. "Think of Hope. Get her home."

There was no trump card I could have played before we had a child, but there was now. Elaine's face tightened with anger and frustration that she couldn't stop whatever it was I was going to do. Or try to do.

"You're going to bait him," she said to me. "With yourself."

"I'm going to end this."

I looked to Nick, fixing a serious look upon him.

"You protect this convoy," I said. "And my family."

"I will, Fletch," he said, uncertain but dedicated to the mission he'd been charged with.

"Go," I said, looking back to my wife. "I have to do this."

There was no joy about her. No way there could be. She simply dropped the pickup into gear and accelerated gently away, holding our daughter as they caught up with the convoy. Nick Withers gave me a small wave, and then they were gone around a bend in the highway.

I was on my own.

But I was not alone. This I knew without a doubt. The rain had stopped and visibility had improved to the point that I could be seen by anyone within a few hundred yards who would bother to look. Olin was out there, watching.

That didn't mean I had to make it easy for him.

Without hesitating I bolted from the highway, running into the woods on the north side of the road. I kept moving, putting distance between myself and where I'd started. If Olin wanted to keep me under observation, with the naked eye or through the scope of his rifle, he would have to work for it. Ten minutes into my move I stopped, taking cover and scanning the path I'd just taken through the trees. A full twenty minutes I waited, listening and watching.

Olin did not follow. No one did.

Confident now that I was not being directly observed, I shifted west, traveling about a half mile before turning south toward the road again. I crossed the highway quickly and moved into the forest, progressing a hundred yards before, again, making sure I was not being trailed. My final push through the stands of grey pines brought me to a place along the banks of the Coquille River. A cautious walk east brought me to a place of concealment where I could see the abandoned outpost, the flag Rebecca had lashed to a post out front still waving lazily in the breeze.

Once more I waited, observing what I could see, and what I could hear.

...*snap*...

The sound was small, emanating from a spot beyond the outpost. Maybe a hundred feet from where I lay prone next to a fallen tree. In the old world I would have written off what I'd heard as an animal stepping on a twig, or a person popping the top of a soda can. Those sounds should not exist in Remote. Not at the moment after it had emptied out.

...*snap*...

Once more the sound came, though this time it was accompanied by a sight as well. Movement. Beyond the outpost. Someone making their way up the slight slope that led to the shoulder of the highway. A man.

A man in a cowboy hat.

Olin...

I held still as he reached the soft edge of the highway and stopped, looking in all directions. My position gave me almost perfect cover. His scan of the area passed right over me, and, after a moment, he continued on across the road to the north.

It was time to make my move. I skirted the bank of the Coquille until I reached where Sandy Creek spilled into the larger tributary. Looking north, I could see where the creek passed beneath the highway, the bridge above shielding any movement from view. I stayed low on the east bank and followed the stream, pausing just before losing the cover of the bridge.

Obscured in the shadow of the overpass, I stayed low and eyed the way ahead. Fifty feet from where I'd stopped the covered bridge still stood, despite having a portion of its upper structure scavenged to repair houses in Remote. There was no movement on the bridge. The same could not be said for the area just to the east of it.

Olin walked into view, his rifle slung as he moved past the old covered bridge and continued along the creek. For a moment as he walked on, the once historic span hid me from view. This was the best chance I might ever have to gain an advantage over the man, and I wasn't going to pass it up.

I left my cover and moved, steady and slow, closing the distance to where Olin had to be beyond the wooden bridge. Staying low and taking each step with care, I passed beneath the structure, my AR up and ready, the safety off, selector set to burst, my eyes looking past the suppressor at the target I'd waited a very long time to have in my sights.

"Olin!"

The man froze where he'd been walking, high on the east bank of Sandy Creek, his back to me.

"Let your rifle fall," I instructed him.

He hesitated, angling his head just a bit toward me.

"I have every reason to shoot you on sight," I reminded him. "Now drop the rifle."

He waited no more, letting the sling slip over his shoulder, the lever action .30-30 dropping into the damp earth at his feet.

"Take four steps forward."

That was precisely what he did. When he was still again I stepped from beneath the covered bridge and made my way up the bank until we were standing at the same level, water rushing just to my left.

"Hands up and turn around."

The man complied, facing me, his expression slack, some part of a surprised, cocky grin curling his lips.

"Slowly, take that jacket off."

Once more he followed the order, revealing what he wore beneath, including a Sig Sauer holstered on his hip.

"Use your thumb and one finger to drop that Sig," I told him.

He did just that, the pistol tumbling into the sloppy muck at his feet.

"Hello, Fletch."

I shook my head at him, the business end of my AR zeroed in on his chest, finger on the trigger.

"You don't get to call me that," I said.

"Right, sorry. Only good friends who you know so well get to use that nick. Friends like Neil."

He had no way out of his situation, and, still, he was taking verbal shots at me. Maybe it was some technique he'd been trained in. Some way to throw an adversary off just enough that a break for freedom could be executed at just the right time.

Or, he was beyond caring and knew what fate lay ahead of him.

"Tell me, Fletch, where's Four Twelve?"

It was my turn to smile. I had to give it to the man, he stayed on mission. His eyes were on the prize they'd been on since that first moment he'd walked into Bandon.

"Where is it?"

"Not gonna happen, Olin."

"That's too-"

We both were jolted by the sharp tremor, earth beneath us seeming as though it was heaving upward, then falling again. Then, without warning, the world turned upside down.

Forty

The east bank of Sandy creek crumbled beneath my feet, sending me tumbling backward into the shallow, icy water. I rolled toward the shore, groping for the weapon that the earthquake and the fall had ripped from my grip.

"You can stop now."

The voice wasn't Olin's. But it was familiar.

"Get up," Ansel told me as he crept from the shadows beneath the covered bridge, AK pointed at me. "Keep your hands in the open."

Above him, standing at the railing of the span, Moira held an identical weapon, stock tucked close to her cheek as she sighted down its receiver and barrel at me.

"Up," Ansel repeated. "I'm not telling you again."

I slowly rose, still standing in the bubbling stream. I brought my hands away from my body and raised them slightly. Olin came down the bank and stepped into the shallow water, retrieving my AR from where I'd dropped it. He released the magazine and kept it in hand as he ejected the chambered round, holding the bolt open to blow into the action several times, clearing any excessive water. That done, he reinserted the magazine and chambered a fresh round, leveling my own weapon at me.

"What did Stalin say?" Olin asked. "Quantity has a quality all its own."

The earthquake had been opportune, but not a game changer. I knew that now. Olin had led me to this spot, into his trap, Dalton's two underlings providing the backup he needed. Ansel stepped close and took my Springfield from its holster, tucking it in his waistband before backing away and taking a position higher on the creek's bank to cover me as Moira remained perched on the bridge.

"In other words, my three beats your one," Olin said.

I took in the sight of the three of them, the dynamic that existed, and had obviously existed, between them more than clear.

"Puppets and puppet master," I said, focusing on Dalton's people. "Ask him what he did to the last man who trusted him."

"We know what he's doing for us," Moira said.

"As soon as we're done with you, it's Dalton's turn," Ansel said.

I turned back to Olin. He tipped my AR to one side and verified that the selector switch was set to burst.

"Is that it, Olin? You told them you'd take out their leader so the colony would be theirs? That's what they get out of this?"

The man didn't answer. He simply grinned at the question I'd posed.

"Ask yourselves this," I said, addressing Ansel and Moira without taking my eyes off the man who'd murdered my lifelong friend. "Who needs who more?"

I sensed a slight shift in Ansel's posture to my right. Maybe he was fidgeting where he stood on the angled bank. Or was he exchanging a look with Moira as they processed the question I'd posed? In the end, whatever reaction they might have had did not matter, as Olin fired a quick burst into Ansel's chest, a second one expertly striking Moira before either could react.

There was no point in moving or making a run for it. By the time Ansel's body had crumpled forward into the creek, and Moira's had flopped backward, a chunk of her forehead blasted onto the covered bridge's rotting rafters, the suppressed muzzle of my AR was directed at me again, the shrouded barrel steaming.

"That was it," I said, only slightly incredulous. "You used them to search for Four-Twelve? You sent them into Bandon to look for it? To push my buttons? To trip me up?"

He smiled and tipped his head toward me.

"That wife of yours knows some field craft, it seems," Olin said. "As for them...they weren't happy with their situation. But they were too afraid to pull the trigger and change it."

Pulling the trigger on Dalton would take some fortitude, I knew. He was a presence, if not a force. And if Ansel and Moira had gone that route on their own, would the rest of the colony coalesce behind them as the new leaders?

"You, the outsider, kill Dalton, and they step in," I said. "But that was never going to happen."

"They seemed to believe it would."

The man smiled, at himself, I thought. At his cleverness. His ability to manipulate others to do his bidding.

"And now?" I asked.

He gave a slight shrug and cocked his head, regarding me as if I was displaying some precious naiveté on purpose. From behind him, mist began to roll in, spilling down the bank of the creek and flowing atop the water, obscuring the world beneath our waists.

"Where is it, Fletch?"

"You think I'm going to tell you?"

"I think you should," Olin said, his smile draining away. "Because if you don't, after I kill you, I'm going to have to pay a visit to that beautiful family of yours."

"You're going to kill me even if I tell you."

To that statement I'd made, he gave a slight nod.

"Where is Four-Twelve?"

I stood in silence. If I were to play my hand and tell him that there was no BA-412, at least not in my possession, it was entirely likely that he would not believe me. Or, if he did, there would be no reason for him to leave me alive.

"Fletch..."

He nudged me verbally to reply, adding some motivation as he brought my AR up and took very deliberate aim at the bridge of my nose. We stared at each other that way for a moment, he down the barrel of my weapon, and I past the suppressor which could, at any second, erupt in a quick flash which my brain would only have a millisecond to process before a bullet would turn out the lights. My lights. Permanently.

"Last chance," Olin said.

I had to make a decision. Bluff. Tell the truth. Or rush him. None were appealing choices. But I chose the latter, readying myself mentally for a quixotic charge which had little chance of success. Not against a man like Olin.

One...

I let myself think of Elaine. My wife. My love.

Two...

And Hope. My daughter. My everything.

Three...

My leg muscles tensed and my hands clenched to fists as my internal countdown ended. It was time to make my move.

I never got the chance. From the right, up on the bank, a fast *whooooosh* sound snapped the silence, and a flash of something, dark and long, rocketed downward at Olin, the man jerking as something struck him.

"Ahhhhh!"

He squeezed off a burst just as I ducked, rounds sailing past my head. So close that I felt a searing hotness upon my right cheek and temple. Olin twisted, the AR falling from his grip, his position allowing me to see the crossbow bolt protruding from both sides of his neck, razor sharp broadhead at its tip half embedded in his right shoulder.

I glanced up the bank of the creek and saw who had fired the saving shot. Dalton. He stood there above the mist-covered waters, empty crossbow in one hand, the other drawing a revolver from his waistband.

Splash!

I looked fast toward the sound. Where I should have seen Olin, there was only empty air and swirling mist where he'd stood. He'd gone under water, using the fog to mask his retreat.

Above, Dalton began sidestepping his way down the bank, coming to my aid.

"No!"

I shouted my admonition to him as I found my Springfield on Ansel's submerged body. After clearing it of water, I fished my AR from the creek where Olin had dropped it and did the same.

"I'm dealing with him," I said, sloshing through the veiled creek toward Dalton.

"I suppose it's good my aim was off, then," he said.

Behind him, just approaching the top of the creek's bank, was Lo. He held his AK at the ready, backing up his leader.

"Just let me handle him," I said.

Dalton glanced to where Ansel's body had fallen near the shore, then to Moira's feet dangling from the edge of the covered bridge. A somber realization washed over him, though it was not born of any grief toward these two.

"Gina wasn't back in town," Dalton said. "She's dead, isn't she."

"She is," I confirmed. "Olin killed her."

Dalton looked to the creek, ground fog creeping up the opposite bank and into the grey woods. There was some connection between him and the woman who'd been shot dead on my porch. Possibly something they'd kept to themselves. Whatever the reason for his solemn reaction, my focus had to stay on what mattered to me—Olin.

"Thank you," I said to the leader of Camas Valley.

He acknowledged my all too inadequate appreciation for saving my life with a simple nod, then I got moving.

* * *

Olin had to have headed north, underwater for a few dozen yards, then using the thickening mist to hide his retreat. I followed what I thought his path would have been, emerging from the creek, dripping and cold as I climbed up the western shore.

The woods that spread out there were shrouded in a wall of fog now, grey on grey. Hardly any visual cues presented themselves which would indicate the man's location. Except the one which stood out stark in the ashen landscape.

Blood.

The bright red splashes lay upon the wet forest floor like Rorschach arrows, pointing the way forward. I followed them, AR sweeping slowly left and right, its suppressed barrel dipped slightly. Every muddy step announced my presence, and there was a distinct possibility that Olin had retained some weapon other than those I'd made him drop, but I continued, one minute, two minutes, three, moving deeper into the woods. Deeper into the fog.

Until I heard the gurgling.

It was breathing, wet and ragged. Close. A dozen yards ahead and to my left. I redirected my aim toward the sound and closed the distance, an image resolving, clearer and clearer with each step I took. A figure. On the ground. Head propped awkwardly against the stout trunk of a towering fir that had long ago succumbed to the blight. It stood now like a tombstone for the man who was not yet dead, but not far from that state, either.

Olin's swimming gaze found me as I finally stopped, a few feet from him, my AR ready to end him.

"Where is it?"

He posed the question with crimson spittle spraying from his mouth. The deadly broadhead had cut some vital veins in his neck, blood pouring down his throat and into his lungs, drowning him from within.

"Where is it?"

Like a dog with a bone, he would not let go. Would not abandon his mission. I wondered if that pointed to him being a man of incredible dedication, or foolhardy determination. Neither mattered.

"Tell me," he said, the final seconds of his life draining away. "Where..."

The information meant nothing to him now, and meant everything. He could do nothing with it, could take no action to retrieve any sample of BA-412 he was directed to, but still he had to know.

"Where..."

He uttered the plea that final time, then coughed, his eyes rolling back and chest rising high, once, twice, before settling to stillness. Gone.

I lowered my AR and stared at the man who'd murdered my friend. Who'd come across the wasted country in search of a prize that could drive a final nail in humanity's coffin. He wanted to know where it was. Wanted me to tell him.

"I don't know," I answered the dead man.

Then I left him to rot and made my way back through the woods and across Sandy Creek. Dalton and Lo were gone, but I wasn't stranded. A short walk to the north of Remote and a quick search led me to what I was looking for.

Gina's motorcycle.

She'd left it after riding cross country from Camas Valley, saying that there was enough of a charge remaining to carry us to over the hills toward Winston. All I needed was for it to get me back to the highway, then west to the coast. I slung my AR and swung a leg over the cycle, studying its simple controls for just a few seconds before activating its electric motor and riding out of the trees.

I was going home.

Forty One

I didn't report in. Didn't stop by the Town Hall, or the garrison headquarters. I passed through a checkpoint that had been set up on the north side of town and rode through the darkened streets until the juice finally gave out on the motorcycle I'd taken. From there I walked, heading for the only place I wanted to be. That I needed to be.

Home.

The screen door was closed, the entry door beyond it open, cool air flowing into the house. I stood on the porch and just looked for a moment. Looked and listened. I saw the inside of my house, of our house, through the fine mesh. Chair and couch and hallway and lamps. But the familiar sights were not what warmed me. What soothed me.

It was what I heard that did that.

Tiny splashes. And the most beautiful voice. Both came from the kitchen, I could tell. Elaine was bathing our daughter. Singing to her. But...

But how could that be? How could my wife be acting so very normal after how we'd separated? Something wasn't right. I reached for the screen door handle, my hand about to grip it and let me into my home, when I was stopped by a sound.

I heard the vehicle pull up across the street behind. I knew before I looked who it was. Schiavo stepped from the Humvee and stood next to it, in the street, staring at me. I sampled the joy within my house for a moment more, then left the porch and crossed the street, meeting the captain next to her vehicle.

She gave me a look, up and down, the expression which accompanied her appraisal of me both apologetic and thankful. And relieved.

"You look like hell, Fletch."

"I don't feel like it."

Caked mud. Ansel's blood, splattered across one side of my face. I'd wiped some off on the ride back from Remote. Other things, though, would not be so easy to cleanse from my body, and my mind.

Despite this, I felt...whole. It was Olin's demise, I knew, that had brought such a feeling of contentment to me. Witnessing his death, bringing an end to the man who'd murdered my friend, who'd threatened my wife and child, was a relief.

"I'm sorry you had to take him on," she said. "Olin."

I'd only been back a few minutes, and had spoken to no one about what had transpired, yet she knew.

"Dalton radioed," Schiavo said, recognizing the mix of surprise and confusion on my face. "He told us what happened."

Dalton...

The man must have reactivated the repeater and transmitter that Ansel and Moira had shut down.

"Elaine knows I'm all right?"

Schiavo nodded. I shook my head, still coming down from the adrenalin rush of all that had happened.

"Dalton," I said.

The leader of Camas Valley had saved me. And he'd watched Olin dispatch two of his lieutenants. He had to have been witness to that event, and what led up to it. Yet he did nothing to intercede. He'd somehow known, or known enough to be suspicious, of both Ansel and Moira. Perhaps he'd developed some belief as to their planned treachery on his own. But I thought not.

"You told him," I said.

There was no specificity to my statement, but from Schiavo's reaction, from the rise of her chin and the quick, shallow breath she took through her nose, it was clear that she knew exactly what I was accusing her of doing.

"You told him that I recognized Ansel after the break-in," I told her. "And that Moira hurt herself getting away."

She shook her head.

"Martin did," she corrected me. "When he went east with the convoy. I asked him to tell Dalton, and only Dalton."

The leader of Camas Valley had been privy to our suspicions when he first visited Remote. He'd even brought Moira with him. That was either a signal that he hadn't yet embraced the accusations, or that he wanted to keep Moira and Ansel believing that they were in his good graces.

"Why didn't you say something? Martin could have told us when we sent Dorothy back with the convoy."

"Dalton swore me to secrecy," Schiavo explained. "I imagine so he could find the proof he needed to take them out with the rest of his peoples' blessing. But Olin took care of that for him."

I'd been saved by the convergence of both luck and design. And by Schiavo's successful attempt at backdoor diplomacy. Had she not opened up to Dalton, there's little chance he, or anyone, would have come to my aid at Sandy Creek.

"You weren't going to tell him," I said, recalling Schiavo's exchange with me outside the Town Hall.

"I wasn't," she said. "Martin changed my mind."

"How?"

"He was absolutely convinced that you were targeted," she said. "His belief in that was unshakable. He was worried, Fletch. About you. So, I modified my view on the matter."

"Modified?'

Her face shrugged over an innocent smile. I was beginning to understand. Not only had Schiavo gone against what she'd told me she was going to do, or not do, she did so without *actually* doing so.

"You had Martin feel him out," I said. "Just see if he wanted any information we'd come across."

"That we'd *stumbled* upon," Schiavo said. "Innocently stumbled upon. The fence and blood, Moira's wound."

"You didn't mention Ansel," I said.

"No. He'd have to make that connection on his own. And, apparently, he did."

She'd made Dalton want the information. Made him seek the full picture himself by having Martin bait him with the vaguest tidbit of what we'd discovered.

"You let him fill in the pieces," I said.

"That's the only way a man like him works. He has to trust his instincts before he trusts what others tell him."

"And you had to trust him," I told Schiavo. "That's not easy to do."

"I imagine he thinks the same about us."

The captain was right. Our world view was shaped by factors that were unimaginable before the blight nearly wiped civilization from the face of the earth. Wariness was a virtue for many, however much it might seem to darken a person's soul.

"For now," Schiavo said, "he's on our side."

I wondered if the alliance was as tenuous as her choice of words implied. Or if it was just complicated, and would continue to be.

That, though, was an issue I would not have to deal with.

On the ride back to Bandon, as I cruised down the narrow highway, past stands of dead trees I could already imagine replaced by towering green new growth in the years and decades to come, the thought of changes began to settle my mind, my heart, my soul.

"I want to see my daughter grow up," I told Schiavo. "I think I've paid my dues to this town for the time being."

My statement, seemingly disconnected from what we'd been discussing, caught the captain off guard.

"What are you saying, Fletch?"

"I just want to be a nobody. I want to open a contracting business and help people put in doors, and hang new windows. I'll finish out my time on the Defense Council and then I'm through."

Schiavo listened, absorbing what I'd just told her. I was no different than the next person in Bandon, except I was. I'd been asked to do things that most others hadn't, and I'd been forced to do what was necessary so that I, and others in town, could survive. I'd volunteered and been drafted on occasion for tasks and missions that would not have existed in the old world, much less conceived. I wasn't a hero, and I wasn't indispensable. But I was an asset. I knew that. I preferred to act rather than wait for others to do the same.

Now, though, my time at the head of the line was up.

"I can't say you don't deserve to live your life as you choose," Schiavo said. "You've earned that right ten times over."

And that was it. There would be some formal discussion with the Council when the time was right. For now, though, it was enough that I'd taken that first step of making my intentions known.

"It's been an interesting time, Fletch."

"Interesting is one word for it, I guess."

For a moment Schiavo turned introspective, grinning through the silence.

"What?"

"From a green Army lieutenant to this," she said. "Now I'm negotiating trade deals."

"Batteries for eggs," I said, recalling the most amusing tenet of our trade agreement with Camas Valley.

"Coup plotters for your life," Schiavo added, looking warmly at me. "The best trade I've ever made."

Her gaze shifted past me. To the house. My house.

"Go start your retirement from public service," she told me.

I didn't need to be told twice. In thirty seconds I was back on the porch, then through the front door, and finally at the doorway where the hall let into the kitchen. Elaine stood at the sink, lifting our daughter from the small plastic tub she'd used to bathe her. I watched my wife for a moment as she dried Hope, then wrapped her in a towel.

Then, she stopped, sensing my presence. She turned, a subdued smile spread across her face.

"Hi, beautiful."

"Hi yourself," Elaine said.

Neither of us made a move toward the other. My wife just stood there, holding our daughter, tiny hands groping past the towel and grabbing at the long black strands of hair hanging tantalizingly close.

"He's dead," Elaine said.

"He is."

"Did you..."

I shook my head. Her face tightened with surprise.

"I watched him die," I told her.

There was no need to offer her any details. No need to expand upon how I'd watched Tyler Olin leave this world. That he was gone was enough, for her, and, for me.

"So it's over."

"Everything is," I said, expanding her statement. "Everything."

"What do you mean?"

"I mean I'm done with all that. All the things we've done until now, we're through. I'm through. From right now until my last breath, I'm yours. Our family is all that matters. Not enemies, not alliances, not missions or battles or anything. It's just you and me and Hope from now on."

A hint of doubt rose in her expression, then settled, a small, relieved smile building.

"Us," Elaine said. "Just *us*?"

"Yes."

She walked to where I stood, lifting our daughter to her shoulder. I bent forward and kissed Hope on the top of her head, then I looked into Elaine's eyes. They glistened with a sheen of happy tears.

"Just us," she said again, as if some dream had come true.

"Forever," I assured her.

Forty Two

The settlers were transported back to Remote just two days after we'd pulled them out. This time, though, they were more on their own than before. The garrison outpost was no longer staffed. Talk amongst those inhabiting the town had centered on turning that now empty building into, of all things, a restaurant.

At first blush such an idea seemed foolish. But when it was considered in light of our communities moving forward, going from surviving to thriving, the existence of such an establishment, however limited its operation might be, would create the potential for commerce. Visitors from Bandon, and, possibly, from Camas Valley, would be free to travel to Remote for, of all things, a bite to eat, something so nostalgically normal.

With the forty settlers returned to Remote, the population of Bandon sank below 800 residents again. Until the beacon began.

One of my final acts as a member of the Defense Council had been to recommend restarting the beacon, our daily broadcast to any who might be listening that Bandon was a safe haven. Despite Dalton's admonishment that we were only inviting trouble, the Council agreed, and, once again, Krista initiated her transmissions, beckoning survivors to join us.

This time, they did.

They came out of the dead woods and on the roads, mostly from the east and south. In ones and twos, and even a group of seven. Survivors. People who now believed that the message they'd been hearing, either directly through radios they'd scavenged, or second hand from other survivors, was genuine. No longer was it polluted by injections of fear that had almost certainly been spread by Olin. There was no consensus as to why he had taken to poisoning the town's reputation. It might have been to isolate us further. Or, possibly, he thought that any person not in our orbit was a potential puppet for him to control at some point, as he had Dorothy.

Dorothy...

Dorothy Quinn. We'd learned her full name as she warmed to the town she'd adopted, and which had welcomed her. Once fearful and broken, she was flourishing now, and spent most of her time helping new arrivals acclimate to life in Bandon. Life that was good, and real. Life that held promise.

Life that held hope.

That we had turned a corner, and were growing, even with the departure of so many to settle in Remote, was deeply satisfying to me. My waning time on the Defense Council had been the most important period of service, I felt. Good things, big things, had been set in motion.

And life at home was as wonderful as I could have imagined. More, actually.

Only a few weeks had passed since I'd come home from Remote for the final time, but the world had righted itself where Elaine and I were concerned. I was her husband, and she was my wife. We were parents of a beautiful child whom we would raise in a world that was, day by day, turning green again.

Our alliance with Camas Valley had solidified, with specialists from each of our communities traveling to the other to provide needed expertise in various fields. Power generation, oil extraction, medicine. We were helping each other. The footprint of humanity's good nature had spread from west to east, and we had every hope that would continue as other survivor colonies were located.

We were moving forward. Not just in baby steps, but in leaps and bounds. There was a confidence building amongst the residents of Bandon. A belief that our tomorrows were going to be bright.

Part Five

Dark Skies

Forty Three

Sally and Nelson Vickers spotted the light while out for a midnight stroll along the beach. He sent her running home to report what they'd seen while he remained to stay focused on the spot of flashing white far offshore.

"Is it still there?" Schiavo asked.

"Right there," Nelson said, pointing to a spot between the rocks rising beyond the surf line.

And there it was. A tiny, hot spot of light, flashing on and off. On and off with some purpose that was more than familiar.

"Private Westin..."

The captain summoned her com expert forward. She'd brought him along, as well as Martin, swinging by my house to pick me up before speeding to the beach. The information that the light was not burning steady, but strobing randomly, had made it abundantly clear that whatever vessel was out there was trying to make contact through code.

"Do you need NVGs?" Schiavo asked.

Westin shook his head, choosing his own standard binoculars over the night vision optics the captain had brought along.

"Let's see what they're saying," Westin said, bringing the binoculars up and focusing in on the distant light.

I looked to Nelson, who stood without his wife, staring out at the pulsing, distant light.

"Sally said you told her to stay at home after she called this in," I said.

Nelson nodded and remained fixed on the staccato flashing where black water met blacker sky.

"She also said you told her to use the phone, not the radio," I recounted, sharing what Schiavo had told me on our way to the beach.

Now Nelson looked at me, concern plain on his face.

"That's Morse code, Fletch," Nelson said, stating the obvious for some effect I didn't yet understand. "To me that says whoever's out there isn't too keen on using the radio, so I figured maybe we shouldn't either."

The man was nearly twice my age, but sharper by a factor of ten. He would make a good addition to the Defense Council, I thought. My time was almost up, and there would be discussions about who to appoint to fill my place, a choice that, as I'd insisted, residents would have to approve through a vote. Elaine had decided to stay as a member, as had the others, but my tenure was coming to an end. Willingly.

"I didn't want Sally down here until we figured out what this means."

"I'd say you made the right move," I told him.

"It's the *Rushmore*," Westin said, drawing all attention to him.

"You're certain?"

Westin lowered the binoculars for a moment and looked to his captain. A smile spread across his still boyish face.

"Positive."

He brought the binoculars back up and focused on the lights again. Lights emanating from the Navy supply ship which had brought us much of what we'd needed to stay alive while farms and fields and forests regenerated. Until one day it came no more, leaving us fearing the worst.

"We need to signal them," Westin said.

Martin looked behind to the Humvee, angled on the sand a few yards away.

"I'll get it pointed in the right direction," Martin said. "We can use the headlights."

It took him less than a minute to reposition the beefy vehicle. He stepped out but remained by the open driver's door.

"Three long flashes, then off," Westin instructed, then zeroed in on the distant lights, waiting through the signal as Martin operated the Humvee's headlights.

"An 'O' for 'okay'," I theorized aloud, and Westin brought one hand briefly off his binoculars and gave me a thumbs up as confirmation.

Just a few seconds after the signal had been sent, the lights out at sea stopped. And stayed dark.

"What happened?" I asked.

"I don't know," Westin answered, still scanning the dark ocean.

Schiavo waited, as the rest of us were. Had the town been made aware of a ship off our coast, even not knowing just which ship it was, the beach would have been flooded with people. Sally Vickers had not shared what she'd seen, clearly in sync with her husband's trepidation concerning the unknown.

"Westin..."

Schiavo calmly prodded her com specialist, her patience thinning.

"Nothing, ma'am."

She shook her head and turned, walking quickly to the Humvee, stepping past her husband to retrieve something from the front seat, returning quickly with the item in hand.

"Who's really out there?" she asked, not expecting an answer from any of us as she raised the stout Night Vision Glasses and dialed in the spot where the light had been.

"What do you see?"

Schiavo didn't answer my question. She passed the NVGs to me so I could see for myself. I did as she had and located the source of the now darkened lights, finding what she just had, a silhouette on the artificially bright horizon, greenish shape unmistakable.

"It is the *Rushmore*," I said.

"Look at her hull forward," Schiavo directed.

I did, and easily found what Schiavo had taken note of. The bow of the ship was unsymmetrical. Graceful lines had turned blunt, even twisted.

"Battle damage," Schiavo said.

I handed the advanced optics back to her. She held them low, having seen enough.

"Why did she stop communication?" Westin wondered aloud to his captain.

"That's not the right question," Martin said, rejoining us from his position by the Humvee. "Why'd they start communicating?"

"She's sending again," Nelson said, pointing past us to the wide, black ocean.

Westin brought his binoculars quickly up and processed the code being sent, watching for a long moment before he briefly lowered the glasses.

"What the hell?"

"Private..."

Westin looked to his commander, more than puzzled.

"Captain, did you have a dog when you were six?"

It took a moment for the weirdness that had swept over Westin to transfer to Schiavo.

"Excuse me?"

"Cap, that's what they're asking," Westin said. "What was Captain Schiavo's dog's name when she was six?"

Schiavo's gaze narrowed down and she looked to me, then to her husband.

"I didn't have a dog," she said. "I had a cat. Her name was Lady."

Martin thought for a moment, then looked out to the ocean which had gone dark again, no lights, the question asked. It was our turn to answer, though what that answer should be, and what the query was truly seeking, seemed to be mired in collective uncertainty.

"Are they trying to identify you?" Martin wondered. "Make sure it's actually you before coming ashore or making further contact?"

"They know enough to know that you're a captain now," Westin said.

When I'd first encountered Schiavo on Mary Island she'd been a lieutenant leading a small contingent of soldiers trying to beat back a rogue Russian incursion along the Alaskan coast. After her actions in Skagway, where she'd led a force which freed hundreds from Kuratov's grip, including helpless children being used as human shields in the pit, word had come that she'd been promoted. Word supposedly from the very top of the chain of command—the President himself.

"If they expect you to be here, then why throw wrong information?" Nelson asked.

Schiavo thought for a moment, as did I. Somehow, whoever was out there knew enough about Captain Angela Schiavo to be confident that the question they were asking would be in the ballpark of correctness, but not on the money. They would also know that an officer of her ability and experience, particularly after all that had happened since the blight struck, would be wary. Or should be.

"Westin," I said, and the trooper looked to me. "Send 'wrong question' to them."

The private waited, shifting his attention to his leader. I knew immediately that Schiavo understood what I was suggesting.

"How would Captain Angela Schiavo really answer them?" I asked her, just to reinforce my point.

She nodded lightly, mostly to herself, the faced Westin.

"Send it," she said.

The private walked to the Humvee where Martin had positioned it and pulsed out the message using the headlights. We waited, scanning the night far beyond the shore as Westin rejoined us and wielded his binoculars again. A second or two later, the lights began again.

"What did they say?" Martin asked.

Westin lowered the binoculars and smiled.

"Who was Lady?"

Schiavo, too, smiled. From an obscure question answered in some compendium of personal information collected on her, a connection had been made.

"That had to be buried deep in the Pentagon somewhere," she said, looking to her com expert. "Give them an answer, private."

Westin hustled to the Humvee to transmit the reply, then returned to zero in on the *Rushmore.*

"Okay, so they know that about me, and they know that I'm here," Schiavo said, trying to comprehend the significance of those two facts. "Why am I suddenly popular?"

Before anyone could offer a guess, educated or otherwise, Westin spoke up.

"They're sending again."

Once more we watched and waited as the message came in.

"Cease all radio communications," Westin said, binoculars glued to his eyes. "Repeat, cease all radio communications."

Schiavo absorbed that directive and looked to me.

"They're not warning about the hiders," I said.

The captain shook her head in agreement. Whatever beacon we'd innocently provided to draw the hidden remnants of civilization to our town, the powers that be aboard the Navy ship would be concerned about larger threats. More profound enemies.

"Further instructions coming soon," Westin translated.

"What instructions?" Martin wondered. "From who? When?"

We waited for some further clarification, but the lights in the darkness pulsed no more. After a moment, Westin lowered the binoculars and looked to us.

"She's pulling away," he said.

Schiavo raised the NVGs and looked out to the *Rushmore*, watching for just a moment before bringing the device down.

"She's heading out to sea," Schiavo confirmed.

The Navy ship hadn't even waited for us to confirm we'd understood her final message. That either meant that those aboard had confidence that we had, or it meant that she'd only come this close to shore with some concern and was now making a hasty retreat.

"Something's not right," Martin said.

I couldn't disagree with him. But to Schiavo, the oddness had an even more ominous familiarity to it.

"We waited for a message before," she said. "Everyone remember how that turned out?"

No one who'd been in Bandon could forget it.

"The Unified Government giving us an ultimatum," Martin said.

"And our answer was war," Nelson recalled.

At that moment, the best we could do was hope, and pray, that history didn't repeat itself.

Forty Four

The roar built an hour before dawn, rumbling over the town, familiar and frightening all at once.

"An aircraft," Elaine said as she roused from the hour of sleep she'd managed after feeding our daughter around five in the morning.

"A big one," I said.

I was already getting up, slipping quickly into my pants and boots. There was a momentary rush of fear, and I was certain Elaine had felt it, too. Having been through the nighttime passage of the Unified Government's drones during the siege, this return of unknown sounds from the sky was, at the very least, disconcerting. Neither of us wanted to consider what it might mean to any degree beyond that.

"Wai—"

I almost said it. Almost told her to wait there, inside with our daughter. But I caught myself.

"We can see from the front yard," I said, correcting my delivery.

Elaine finished dressing, then the both of us gave a quick look in on our still sleeping daughter and grabbed our long weapons from the front closet before heading out.

There was only the barest hint of the new day to the east, a trickle of light blue outlining the treetops, but the sky in all other directions was pure black flecked by flickering stars and bright points of light that were Jupiter and Mars. No moon hung above, leaving the fading night to seem, for a while at least, as total as it had been before we'd been awakened.

"It's from the south," Elaine said.

She was right. And it was coming closer, the sound changing as it did, the familiar whine of jet engines rising.

"Fletch!"

Dave Arndt came jogging toward us from his place up the block. His Remington pump was slung across his back, untied laces of his boots whipping about with each hurried step.

"What do you think it is?" he asked.

"I'd rather know who it is," Elaine said, letting her MP5 hang at her side from its sling.

We were all armed and ready, as were most people spilling onto the street. The unknown had often presented itself in ways that later turned out to be threatening. There was a reasonable wariness toward the approaching aircraft.

To me, though, its appearance seemed too coincidental. The arrival of the *Rushmore* offshore just over twenty four hours earlier might not be related, but I didn't think so. Its sudden and unexplained retreat from the coast had left those of us who'd witnessed it unsure of the reason for its visit. The coded messages flashed could be thought of as some mission it was performing.

Or they might have been a ruse to confirm that our military commander was present for targeting, not for talking.

"These aren't going to do anything against it," I said, briefly lifting my AR.

"That thing's a monster," Dave said.

He was not wrong. And as the craft drew closer and closer, flying what could only be described as a bit above treetop level, we began to feel its approach, the rumble buzzing up from the earth below and through our feet.

"Here it comes," Dave said.

Elaine reached out and took my hand as the shadow the craft made against the sky grew, and grew, its wings seeming like those of some predatory bird sweeping down upon its prey.

"Jesus!"

Dave shouted the exclamation and slammed his hands over his ears, the big jet streaking almost directly overhead, its deafening roar shaking any who had not already risen out of their beds. I cringed, straining to get a better look at the plane, but could only glimpse minimal details from its silhouette. Four engines hung beneath its wings, which sprouted from a wide, long fuselage. As I turned to keep tracking its progress north, I saw Elaine sprinting away from where we stood, bounding up the steps and into the house, obviously worried that the unexpected noise of the pass directly overhead had startled our daughter from her sleep.

"What the hell's going on, Fletch?"

I had no answer for Dave. Even if I'd wanted to hazard some guess connecting the overflight with what a few of us had seen the previous day, I couldn't. Word of the *Rushmore*'s reappearance hadn't leaked from the small circle which was privy to that knowledge. This, though, was about as far from a secret as a thing could be.

"I'm not sure, Dave."

The sound receded, then seemed to sweep west, out over the Pacific.

"It's turning," Dave said.

"Coming back for another pass," I suggested.

Before Dave could agree or offer a counter to what I'd said, a Humvee came fast around the corner up the block and pulled to a sliding stop next to my pickup at the curb. Schiavo, Martin, and Westin got out and joined me where our yard met the sidewalk.

"It's a seven-forty-seven," Martin said.

"You're sure?" I asked.

"Saw enough of that forward hump to know," he told me.

"Someone got a commercial bird up," Westin said.

To that, Schiavo shook her head, the expression tinged with a hint of suspicious uncertainty.

"I don't think so," she said.

Elaine came back out, Hope bundled tight and held against her chest. She was fussing, maybe frightened. The only solace I took after noting that was the belief that no imprint of this terrifying memory would last. The blissful ignorance of newborn life would shield her from that.

"He's coming around," Martin said.

Next to him, Westin brought up his binoculars and focused in on the aircraft as it returned to a path over land to the south, turning north again, to repeat its previous track, it seemed.

"What does this guy want?" Dave wondered aloud.

As it turned out, it wasn't what the pilot wanted—it was what he wanted us to see.

"His lights are on," Westin said, taking his eyes from the binoculars for a moment to look to his captain. "And he's flashing them."

Schiavo nodded and Westin refocused through the binoculars to verify what most of us were already thinking—Morse.

"Further instructions," Martin said, parroting part of the message the *Rushmore* had left us with.

The aircraft continued to speed toward us, its landing lights pulsing, their brilliance still enough to cut through the growing light from the dawn breaking to our left.

"Specialist..."

Schiavo's prompting did not draw Westin from his deciphering. He remained zeroed in on the approaching aircraft as he relayed what he was seeing.

"They're repeating the same message over and over," the young soldier said. "Send delegation to PDX ASAP."

"PDX is Portland International Airport," Elaine said.

"That may not even exist anymore," Martin said.

There was no doubt that the city had been devastated. On our trip north along the coast, we'd seen the mouth of the Columbia River engulfed in flames from a tanker that had run aground. Sixty miles upriver, there was no doubt that Portland had suffered fires just as bad.

But runways wouldn't burn. The airport might still be usable. It was possible, maybe even likely, that the aircraft had scouted their intended landing point prior to heading south toward our location.

"A delegation," Martin said. "That sounds...official."

"Right," Dave agreed. "But a delegation to meet who?"

A moment later, it became unnecessary to offer an answer to my neighbor. The aircraft shifted its course to the west, cruising out over the Pacific, its track parallel to the coast, just a few hundred yards from the beach. The rising sun, just peeking over the dead woods to the east, spread a clear, warming light across the landscape, shining bright upon the plane's blue and white fuselage.

"Is that..."

Westin asked the truncated question, though he knew the answer. We all did. Everyone could see with the naked eye what had just flown over Bandon.

"That's Air Force One," I said.

The majestic plane, once a symbol of American power and influence, soared north, gaining altitude. We watched it, speechless, until it climbed into a wall of clouds somewhere over Coos Bay, and was gone.

Schiavo hadn't said a word since the plane made its low pass. A very purposeful pass with no other reason than to make its identity obvious to all who would be looking.

Forty Five

"Martin is going with me," Schiavo said.

We stood on the sidewalk in front of the Town Hall. When the captain had asked me to stay after the brief meeting of the Defense Council, where she'd outlined her plans to take a three person team to Portland, I'd suggested that Elaine take our pickup home to relieve Grace and Krista, who'd been gracious enough to watch Hope while also wrangling Brandon. My wife did not protest, though both she and I knew what was going to transpire once Schiavo and I were alone.

"It seems I keep asking you the same thing," she said. "Just under different circumstances. I wouldn't if there was a better alternative, but...I'd like you to go with us."

She could have made the same request at the meeting, though I knew why she did not. There was no doubt that Martin would be going with her. Even if she wanted him to remain in Bandon, he would ignore such a desire. If she was setting out across potential dangerous territory, unexplored since the blight, he was going to be at her side. The converse of that was why Schiavo hadn't broached the makeup of her team inside. Already she'd had me go to Remote to help get the settlement up and running, a mission which Elaine had joined after a flourish of tension between us. Here, though, there was no chance that my wife could accompany me on a trek so far from Bandon with our infant daughter in tow. I would not allow that even if it were possible.

"I could really use you, Fletch," she said. "You've been out there, in places that have been decimated. You've gone to hell and found your way back. I need that. None of my guys have that skillset."

I'd crossed the wastelands with Neil and Elaine, then travelled north to Alaska. Schiavo and her unit had only been with us on that latter journey, most of which was completed on the water. This would be different, and she knew that. Towns and cities battered by the collapse of civilization were likely to be passable only with difficulty. And that assumed they were emptied out.

But, as we'd learned by the appearance of a community in Camas Valley, not to mention the smaller clans of hiders scattered about the countryside, life had found a way to persevere. Unlike the passive whales broaching off the coast, any humans we encountered would be equally as likely to see us as threats, or as opportunities. I'd been faced with those very people between here and Cheyenne. My knowledge and experience in dealing with such encounters, or avoiding them altogether, would be invaluable to Schiavo.

But my ultimate responsibility wasn't to her. Or to the rendezvous in Portland with whoever was aboard Air Force One. My focus was here. On my family. They needed me, and I had to be there for them.

"I can't," I told her.

She didn't react for a moment. There was every chance she'd anticipated this answer from me. The request still had to be made, I understood, but I sensed she similarly could not question my response.

"Of course," she said.

"At some point, someone else has to step up," I said, the words feeling selfish as I spoke them. "That sounds terrible, like no one's done anything, but..."

"You've done a lot, Fletch," Schiavo said, not challenging my assertion, or belittling my inadequate words. "You've done enough."

Enough...

I wondered, in this world, if such a concept could last for very long. There was no stopping. No retiring. Everyone had a role, even if it was self-defined. Some, like Schiavo, like Martin, like mayor and doctor Everett Allen, were called upon to do what needed to be done.

Then, there were people like me. Men and women who'd stumbled into some level of respect because we fought to survive, and fought so others could. I'd done what had to be done, just as Elaine had, and Grace. And Neil.

Now, though, the sense that what I'd done, what we'd done, had reached some limit was a known belief on my part. I could do more, but at what cost, to me and to my family? This was a world of heroics without heroes, because simply living to see the most recent sunrise was an act of utter heroism. Anyone who'd glimpsed the warm colors of the new day had overcome all that man and nature had thrown at them to do so. I was not special. I was just stubborn, like every person who hadn't given up when all around them turned grey and died.

"I'm sorry," I told her, but she shook her head, smiling.

"You shouldn't be," she said. "I'll find a third person and we'll make it."

"Of course you will."

Captain Angela Schiavo said no more. She simply returned to the Town Hall, most certainly to begin searching for the person who would take the place she'd hoped I would fill.

For a brief instant as I realized that, I felt a pang of regret. Not that I would be here, with Elaine and Hope, but because someone else would fill a spot that I would have almost naturally inhabited. That, though, was my choice. I was at peace with it.

For now.

Forty Six

The Humvee was loaded with supplies and the small trailer it pulled held still more, enough to sustain the three who would travel to Portland for two weeks, if necessary. I would not be among them.

"Every day at two we'll attempt direct radio contact," Schiavo said.

We...

She'd chosen her third person, though I knew for a fact he'd volunteered when he learned there was a place open on the expedition. Carter Laws had turned eighteen while beginning his training to become a soldier in the United States Army, completing an abbreviated course of study designed and implemented by Sergeant Lorenzen. That the young man was originally from Portland made clear that there was a more personal reason for his offer to join Schiavo and Martin on their trek.

His mother.

She'd disappeared while scavenging food in the city during the initial chaos following the blight, leading him to set off in search of safety on his own. He'd found it in Bandon. And, now, so had another.

Dorothy Quinn. She, too, had survived, both with others and on her own. And, in Carter's mind, if she could make it, then his mother might have as well.

This was not a mission to find and rescue her. He knew and accepted that. This journey was, apparently, requested by the nation's surviving leadership. Carter, though, had in the back of his mind that there might be some small chance that, when reaching the city on the Columbia River, his mother might be there, alive and waiting.

It wasn't a longshot. It was a near impossibility. But the newly minted private, wearing a spare uniform that had to be tailored down to his diminutive frame from what had been brought in by the *Rushmore* on her first visit, had hope that she could still be alive. Blind hope, maybe, but I knew firsthand how real and powerful that insistence to hang on could be.

"You listen to the captain," Sergeant Lorenzen told Carter as he slid behind the wheel of the Humvee. "She's the smartest officer I've ever known. The toughest, too."

Schiavo gave her sergeant a look of appreciation and came around the front of the vehicle to face him. He came to attention and saluted her. She returned the show of respect, then offered her hand.

"Don't burn the place down, Paul," she said as he shook her hand.

"Not a chance, ma'am."

Schiavo took the seat next to Private Carter Laws. Martin hesitated just a moment, looking to me. I stood with Elaine and our daughter, Grace with us, her very active youngest at home being watched, or corralled, by his big sister.

"If we're not back in a week, will you do me a favor?"

"Of course, Martin," I said.

"Micah's birthday," he said, making himself smile. "Can you stop by the cemetery and tell him happy birthday for me?"

"We'll all go," Elaine said.

"All of us," Grace agreed.

The man thanked us with a look that meant more than words. Beyond him, in the passenger seat, Schiavo watched the exchange, keeping her emotions in check with some effort.

"Get back safe," I said.

"That's the plan," Martin assured me.

He climbed into the seat behind Carter, reaching forward to put a hand briefly on his wife's shoulder before closing the door.

"Get us moving, private," Schiavo said.

Carter gave us a brief wave and pulled away. A few dozen people had gathered for the departure, each wishing those departing swift and trouble free travels.

"Fletch..."

It was Lorenzen. He spoke my name without ever taking his eyes off the Humvee as it cruised away from us.

"Yeah?"

"How long?" he asked. "There and back? You know what it's like out there. So how long?"

The sergeant was giving me the same credit Schiavo had when asking me to be part of the expedition, believing that my time crossing the wastelands to Cheyenne gave me unique insight. It might, but that was a while ago now. What the trio departing might face could be easier by an order of magnitude. Or worse.

I had to give him something, though. He was concerned, though he would likely brand what he was feeling just a compelling curiosity.

"Four, five days there," I said. "A day to do their business, if that's reasonable."

"And the same back?"

"Right," I told Lorenzen.

"So eleven days," he said.

"That should be enough," I agreed.

He thought for a moment, as if performing some calculation that had nothing to do with math, but with reality. The reality of the world in which we lived.

"So if they're not back in two weeks?" he asked.

"I don't know, Paul."

"They'll be back," Elaine told him.

Lorenzen looked to her, wanting to believe that, but I could tell there was some serious doubt working on the man.

"I hope so," Lorenzen said. "I just..."

"What?" I asked him.

"I don't have a great feeling about this," he said. "I told the captain I should go with her, not Carter. But she wouldn't have it."

"She needs a leader here," I reminded him.

He nodded grimly.

"That's exactly how she put it," Lorenzen said. "Except the way she said it, it seemed like...like maybe she saw it as a permanent sort of thing."

I looked down the street and saw the Humvee following the sweep of the road, disappearing from sight. Eleven days, I'd suggested. By then we should see our friends again. By then we should know what the rendezvous in Portland had been about.

Eleven days...

A lot could happen in that span of time. Good and bad. Or disastrous.

Forty Seven

Two days after the mission to Portland departed, at thirty two minutes past five in the morning, the earth shook with a ferocity none of us had ever experienced.

"Get the baby!"

Elaine shouted to me as I rounded the end of our bed, the sound of items crashing to the floor throughout the house ringing in the night. I bounced off the swaying doorframe and crossed the hallway, our daughter wailing in her room, the violent movement jolting her from a blissful sleep. I grabbed the edge of the crib and tried to steady it as my wife followed me in, falling over the changing table as it toppled.

"Are you okay?"

"I'm fine," she said, scrambling to her feet and taking our daughter from her crib.

"We've gotta get out of here," I said, a large crack spreading across the plastered ceiling.

A sharp jolt amidst the rolling threw Elaine against the wall. She wrapped our daughter in a tight hug to protect her as I reached out and pulled the both of them close.

"Front door!"

I yelled the direction and guided my wife and daughter into the hallway. Leftover artwork from the home's previous owner fell from simple mountings and crashed to the hardwood floor, spreading glass. In the living room there would be more of the same, if the sounds of destruction were any indication. Lamps had fallen. Bulbs were shattered. Vases with actual living flowers had been jostled from their places on tables and the mantle to break into hundreds of jagged ceramic shards.

"Stay here!"

Elaine planted herself between the narrow hallway walls as the building rocked and leapt around us. I made my way back into our bedroom, grabbing the bedposts to steady myself before dropping to the floor to retrieve what we should have grabbed in the first place—our shoes. I groped around in the near darkness, the closet door flying open as the contents of shelves within spilled and virtually exploded out into the room.

"Eric!"

If I had to, I would run across broken glass with my wife and daughter in my arms, but I was hoping not to have to.

"Got them!"

I found my low boots first, and Elaine's tennis shoes a few seconds later, bolting back into the hallway as the window in our bedroom shattered from the frame racking.

"Give me your feet," I told Elaine, jamming more than slipping her shoes onto them.

"This is too long," she said to me, the shaking going on and on.

"I know."

I shoved my feet into my boots and helped Elaine up, keeping a wide stance for balance as we walked down the hallway. For an instant the awful nightmare I'd had flashed in my head, with Olin blocking our way from leaving our burning house. This was not that, though it was terrifying all by itself.

"Look out!"

An armoire to the left of the door to the kitchen shifted and tipped, upper half breaking free of the ornate lower, glass inset in the doors cracking into dozens of glinting shards. I shoved the fallen piece of furniture aside and reached back for Elaine, taking hold of her sweatshirt, its shoulder bunched in my hand as I steadied her against the continued shaking.

"Eric!"

I turned just as her warning reached me, but not in time to avoid the door of the coat closet from slapping my side as it swung violently on its hinges. The impact was sharp and quick, knocking the breath from me momentarily. But I powered through the pain, pinning the door against the jamb with my body as I pulled my wife and daughter through the debris littering the space and to the exit.

Dozens of neighbors were already in their yards, some in the street, an old lamppost down the block toppled, blocking half of the avenue.

"Fletch!"

It was Dave Arndt. He had his shotgun across his back and a go bag in hand, his response far more dialed in than my own. He had no family to immediately worry about, though, his bachelor situation conducive to getting out and gearing up with haste.

But he hadn't emerged unscathed. The thin trickle of blood from a small cut above his eye made that apparent.

"Dave, are you okay?"

He dragged a sleeve across the wound and nodded.

"Stupid mirror flew off the wall," he said. "It's nothing. Elaine, how's the baby?"

"She alive," my wife said, almost choking on the mix of emotion and adrenalin.

The swaying beneath our feet eased, the earth stilling.

"I'm going to check on Mrs. Traeger," Dave said, then spun and jogged off toward our elderly neighbor's house.

He only made it ten steps before the siren sounded, wailing from atop speakers positioned on poles in the downtown area.

"Tsunami!"

One of our neighbors shouted the warning, loud enough that everyone within ten houses could hear. Dave Arndt, after pausing at the sound, sprinted now toward our elderly neighbor's house.

"It's a contingency," I said, looking to Elaine.

She knew this as well as I did. The Defense Council had discussed reactivating the tsunami warning system in light of the continuing seismic activity, though any sensors out at sea which could confirm the approach of a devastating wave were no longer monitored, if they were still working at all.

"Let's get moving," she said.

* * *

Residents streamed along roads which had been marked as Tsunami evacuation routes long before the blight was even a glint in some laboratory madman's eye. Those who were not as mobile, or mobile at all, were assisted by neighbors who'd agreed, as part of the town's emergency plan, to accompany those in need. A half an hour before dawn broke, with the ocean a black expanse to the west, the exodus to safety had been completed.

"No one is missing?" Lorenzen asked.

"So far, it looks like everyone is accounted for," Enderson reported, checking a thick clipboard he carried. "We just have two dozen to the north moving livestock, but they're in communication with Westin by radio."

"If the wave shows, you see that he tells them to haul their butts to high ground," the sergeant told him. "People before animals."

"Already told him just that."

Lorenzen nodded, then shook his head.

"I hope they're all right," he said.

There was no need to specify who he was referring to. Nearly forty eight hours ago the expedition to Portland had left. Under old world conditions they would have arrived by now. But this wasn't that world. They could be fifty miles from Bandon, or a hundred and fifty. There was no way to know. The last radio contact with them had been almost thirty six hours earlier, when they were just entering Reedsport, a bit over thirty miles distant. After that, simple line of sight had prevented any reliable radio signal to be received, even using the Camas Valley repeater.

"They'd be inland by now," I said. "Any tsunami won't affect them."

"Yeah," Lorenzen said, half confident in his agreement at best. "As long as they weren't on a bridge when it hit."

"They were probably sacked out," Elaine reassured him, our daughter deep asleep in her arms. "Like the rest of us."

Grace waded through a knot of residents who had gathered at our vantage point, which held a clear view of the Pacific. Brandon's drowsy head lay on her shoulder, pouting at the commotion all around.

"Where's Krista?" Elaine asked her.

"She's back there with Private Westin setting up the portable radio," Grace answered.

The radio blackout that the *Rushmore* had signaled about could not be absolute. We'd needed to communicate with the expedition heading north, and hopefully would again. This, though, required that any restrictions be lifted. Being able to communicate via radio was vital after a disaster such as what we'd just been through. And what might be yet to come.

"The hospital was cleared out," Grace shared. "Clay is with Mr. Porter in the ambulance."

Ted Porter, the unfortunate recipient of a broken leg during a game of touch football, was the only admitted patient to be removed. Beyond that bit of information that Grace shared, though, was something else she said. How she referred to Commander Genesee. As Clay.

"Good," Sgt. Lorenzen commented, waving Hart over when the medic was within sight.

"Yes, Sergeant?"

"Has Westin been able to reach Remote?"

"No," Hart answered. "He said he can't even reach the repeater."

The repeater in Camas Valley, which took advantage of their transmission tower, could very well have been knocked out by the quake. Or lost power. In either event, without that electronic relay, no signal could get in or out of the settlement.

"When this passes, I want you to take a volunteer with you out to Remote to check on any casualties and damage. If you can, do the same in Camas Valley."

"Got it, Sarge. And two trucks of supplies are in the safe zone."

Lorenzen nodded, but wasn't satisfied.

"This is a wakeup call," he said.

"We need a cache of supplies already in the safe zone," I said, agreeing.

"Let's make that agenda item number one," Lorenzen said, scanning the crowd. "Is the mayor anywhere close?"

"I'll find him," Enderson said, setting off in search of the town's leader.

Satisfied that all Bandon's residents were accounted for, Lorenzen shifted his attention west. Next to him, Hart brought a pair of binoculars to his eyes and scanned the choppy waters stretching to the horizon and beyond.

"That was at least a seven," Elaine said, giving the earthquake we'd all just experienced a guestimate on the Richter scale. "I've been through fives, and they were nothing compared to this one."

There was no United States Geological Survey to determine and broadcast the actual magnitude of the quake, nor its epicenter. If it was as large as Elaine was suggesting, and located on the seabed in the distance, a catastrophic tsunami was a very real possibility.

But none came. We watched the Pacific for almost an hour, waiting for a rising wall of water to inundate the lowest areas of the town. The ocean was as it always was, churning and lovely. No outflow of tides to feed any coming tsunami materialized. We'd all been spared.

Then, someone looked to the northeast.

"My God..."

It was Dave Arndt, my neighbor, whose almost quiet exclamation turned our heads. In ones and twos at first. Then by the dozens we looked until every soul in Bandon was staring at the column of smoke rising into the dawn sky, dark and grey, unlike the product of any fire I'd ever seen. Because it was not that at all.

"That's an ash cloud," I said.

As a boy in Montana I'd listened as my father told tales of the rain of gritty pumice ejected by Mount St. Helens, hundreds of miles from my childhood home. I was just a baby then, but he'd saved articles and pictures of the event, and my mother kept a small jar of the ash that had coated the city, inches deep in places. What we were witnessing, I knew, was a volcanic eruption.

"By direction that has to be Mt. Hood," Elaine said.

"Isn't that dormant?" Hart asked.

"Dormant doesn't mean dead," Lorenzen reminded his medic.

"That's what all the earthquakes were," Elaine said. "It was rumbling back to life."

I turned to Lorenzen as worried chatter spread through the gathered residents.

"You can see Mt. Hood from Portland," I told the sergeant.

The implication of what I was saying was plain to both of us. Three of our people were heading right into what might well be termed hell on earth.

"They can't be there by now," he said. "But they're a lot closer to the eruption than we are."

"So is Air Force One," Elaine said.

And, we had to assume, so was the President.

"Get Westin up here," Lorenzen told Hart.

The medic dashed away through the crowd in search of the unit's communications specialist.

"If we get a wind from the north," Dave Arndt said.

That very weather condition had brought the freak blizzard to Bandon just weeks ago. The breeze now was from the west. The *north*west. If that shifted to what my neighbor was speaking of, ash could fall upon our town, piling on roofs to the point of structural collapse. Crops could be devastated. Livestock would choke on the fine material being spewed two hundred miles distant.

"That ash column has to be fifty thousand feet tall," I said.

"Sixty," Grace corrected me, explaining when she noticed me looking. "College geography. We're not even seeing the bottom thirty thousand feet of the column."

I understood what she was saying. Just like with our radios, the curvature of the earth limited line of sight. For something as distant as Mount Hood, we would only be seeing the highest part of the rising tower of smoke and ash.

"Sarge..."

Lorenzen turned to Westin as he joined us.

"Try to contact the captain."

"Already am," Westin told the sergeant, then shook his head. "If we couldn't hear them last night, hearing us today probably isn't going to happen."

"Keep trying," Lorenzen said, and Westin hurried back to the portable radio he'd set up.

Elaine put a hand on my arm and I looked to her.

"Eric, what will they do?"

I wanted to say that Angela, Martin, and Carter would turn back. That would be the logical course of action to preserve themselves. As every life in this world was precious beyond mere numbers, prudence would dictate that.

But Schiavo was also a soldier. An officer. And she would be thinking much the same things that we had, including considering the fact that the plane presumably carrying the President of the United States almost certainly was within the danger zone of the eruption. A quake feeling like a seven as far away as we were must have been simply devastating to Portland and areas surrounding it.

"They'll keep going," I told Elaine.

"That could be suicide," Grace said.

I nodded. It could be just that. But her mission had been to get to Portland to meet Air Force One. Now, in her mind, it very well could be that she believed their trek had turned into a rescue mission of incalculable importance.

"We should get people back to their houses," Mayor Allen said as he arrived with Corporal Enderson. "It's cold and, well, preparations are going to need to be made."

"Agreed," Sgt. Lorenzen said.

"Damage is going to need to be repaired," Mayor Allen said. "And buildings are going to need to be readied for any ash cloud."

I listened to the discussion between the senior military leader in Bandon and the political leader. Others around them chimed in as they talked about necessities and plans and critical steps to take, Elaine and Grace prominent among those contributing.

I said nothing. My time on the Defense Council was almost up. Those who'd been used to my participation at times such as these had weaned themselves from the expectation that I would be front and center, leading the charge to deal with the devastation.

And with our missing friends.

They were out there, in danger. Maybe in more distress than we could imagine. And I was here, where I'd wanted to be. Relatively safe.

"We've got to get them," I said, blurting out the forceful directive, then correcting it somewhat. "Someone has to."

Those who'd been talking looked to me. As did Elaine. She was worried, sensing that the part of my character which had existed before the blight, and developed further during the ravages of its worst times, was rising once more, despite my promise and efforts to step back from the leadership position that had come naturally to me.

"Someone," I repeated.

But she didn't look away from me, her expression going slack with fear, and with realization. She knew, and I knew, that the only someone I was truly speaking of was me.

"We'll wait," Enderson said. "To see if any communication works."

"It won't," I told him.

"No," Elaine said. "It won't."

My wife reached with her free hand and put her palm to my cheek. In that touch I felt all that I needed to from her—love, tenderness, support.

And agreement.

"You have to go," she said to me.

I nodded against her touch and turned, looking to the monstrous cloud now spreading across the sky. I'd promised to never leave my wife and daughter again. Now, I was backing away from that, and I would be heading into the maelstrom which had spawned the tower of burning ash that filled the northern sky.

"Are you sure, Fletch?" Enderson asked me.

I looked to him and shook my head, not certain about anything. Especially the outcome of any attempt to reach our expedition.

"But we have to try," I said.

Elaine stepped close. I wrapped my arms around her and our daughter and held them, just held them, wanting to remember the realness of the feeling. In case it was the last time.

Thank You

I hope you enjoyed *Avenger*. Please look for other books in *The Bugging Out Series*.

About The Author

Noah Mann lives in the West and has been involved in personal survival and disaster preparedness for more than two decades. He has extensive training in firearms, as well as urban and wilderness Search & Rescue operations, including tracking and the application of technology in victim searches.